To Jake, *upon ...*
Lily Belle —

THE ROCK CREEK SHAMAN

By

Joyce Edelson

*I hope you enjoy this
spiritual journey.
Love,
Aunt
Joyce*

E

THE ROCK CREEK SHAMAN

To order *The Rock Creek Shaman*, go to: www.JoyceEdelson.com,
or send check/money order to:
Joyce Edelson, P.O. Box 434, Riva, MD 21140-0434
Please enclose check or money order for: $16.98, plus $1.02 Maryland sales tax,
plus $6.00 Shipping and Handling—for a total amount of **$24.00**. This amount
applies only for U.S. shipments not including Hawaii or Puerto Rico.
Author accepts e-mail: JoyceEdelson@gmail.com

ISBN 978-0-9823354-0-6
Library of Congress Control Number: 2009921935

Published by:

BAY MEDIA, INC.
550M Ritchie Highway, #271
Severna Park, MD 21146
Tel: 410-647-8402 • Fax: 410-544-4640
Web site: www.baymed.com

THE ROCK CREEK SHAMAN

By Joyce Edelson

Contents

Acknowledgements

Permit me a brief acknowledgement of those who provided invaluable feedback in getting this story ready for publication. My appreciation and gratitude to all of them is unlimited. Each can claim part ownership of this book:

My friends: Amber At Lee (and her high school English class and their teacher), Ray Ehrle, Jane Frantzich, Kathy and Libby Hennemuth, Bob Loisselle, Jane and Frank Matanzo, Dana Owen, and Jeremy Stevenson.

My professional colleagues: Terri Boddorff, Betsy Earley, Brenda Gracely, Marge Hulbert, Phyllis Saroff, and Pat Troy.

My entire family: Especially my partner, Don Gantzer, and my son, Doug, have been encouraging and supportive during each facet of the research and writing of this book, for which I remain eternally grateful. This includes our dog, Tahoe, and three cats, Bass, Ale, and Harp. Ale often sat with me while I created this story, occasionally pawing at some of the illustrated animals on the screen. They all participate in my meditation circle.

Historical Research:
I spent a lot of time and effort researching the historical background for the setting of this book. I was as diligent as I knew how to be in portraying the historical facts accurately. If there are any errors, I would ask that you forgive any oversight, and remember that this is a work of fiction. The characters and plot are a figment of my dreams and imagination. But please don't let War-ne-la or her family in on that "little" secret. They think they're real people. Actually, I think so too—and that's my "bigger" secret.

A Korean Proverb:
Though the gods give shamans their miraculous powers, shamans must learn the technique of invoking them.

This is the story of a young girl who learns how to invoke her powers.

B.I.G.

Charitable donation to Books for International Goodwill (B.I.G.) from sale proceeds of The Rock Creek Shaman:
One dollar ($1.00) from the sale of each copy of The Rock Creek Shaman book will be donated to Books for International Goodwill (B.I.G.)–(www.big-books.org). Please take a moment to review the website.

It is the signature project of the Parole (Annapolis) Rotary Club in Maryland, of which I am a past president. I have long been a staunch B.I.G. supporter, and serve as a member of its Board of Trustees. I also supervise the retail portion of the B.I.G. operation. B.I.G. holds eight retail sales a year to help fund its non-profit operation. B.I.G. sends elementary through college textbooks, children's, adult fiction and non-fiction books to those who most need them for supplementing sparsely equipped school and community libraries in poor areas everywhere in the world, including many places in the United States.

B.I.G.'s Motto: Keeping Books Alive.

Joyce Edelson

Permission to Reprint

Prologue

To the casual observer, we were a perfectly normal family. During my adolescence, a mysterious force pointed me toward a spiritual vision quest in the Blue Ridge Mountains of Virginia, a few hours' drive west of Washington, D.C., where I grew up. The beginning steps of this spiritual path were filled with adversity and conflict. My travels extended all around the world and nearly claimed my life several times.

My parents named me **War-ne-la**, after a female shaman from my mother's Kwakiutl Tribe of British Columbia, Canada. On my father's side, I'm part Australian Aborigine. I have long black curly hair, dark skin and piercing blue eyes. That contrast is the only outwardly visible characteristic that might set me apart from anyone else.

In the summer before my high school senior year, a judge was murdered in our city, and the identity of the murderer was revealed to me during an inner shamanic journey. I felt bound to reveal his identity to the court, which then subpoenaed as trial exhibits all the handwritten journals of my inner shamanic journeys. Recently the court returned my journals, and I re-read them. You are about to learn why those journals were written and the circumstances surrounding them. Until now, nobody else knew the whole story of my childhood that I'm relating to you. I've written this story to satisfy the need to incorporate back into my being the public exposure of my early spiritual world. As a shaman, my calling is to heal. Sharing this story has brought about my own healing and closure to that chapter of my life. I'm glad to have you along for this journey, and I hope you'll enjoy the trip. We'll speak again at the end.

Chapter One
Railroading Across the Canadian Rocky Mountains

Perhaps the dream about the train trip and robbery when I was six years old was the beginning of my awareness that I, **War-ne-la Medici**, saw and heard things differently from others. That particular dream is the earliest one I can remember that actually happened in my real life.

My parents, **Dominic** and **Kathy Wallas Medici**, and I were taking a trip on the Canadian-Pacific Railroad across the Rocky Mountains of Canada. The dream prior to the trip had been scary because our lives had been threatened. In the dream, my parents had been held at gunpoint by someone trying to steal their wallets. I hadn't told my parents about the dream and had pretty much forgotten about it; that is, until the second day into the trip.

We had been riding on the train, quietly enjoying the wildlife and beautiful scenery of a part of Canada none of us had ever seen. An older gentleman joined my parents and me at our table. He told us he traveled the railroad line as a goodwill ambassador, or ombudsman. My mother explained, "That means his job is to take care of whatever the railroad needs to keep everything running smoothly." I recognized the man because he had been in my dream. I gradually began to remember other things from my dream. Fear for our safety began to surround me. Shortly after that first meeting, the older gentleman asked my father if he could have a word with him. The two of them left the table and spoke in low voices in the corner of the railroad car.

We were scheduled to stop at a small town for a bit of shopping in its historic general store. Because I had dreamed there would be bandits near the store and someone would demand they hand over their valuables, I said in a low voice, "Mama and Papa, please lock your wallets in the bags overhead before we leave the train, just in case." I knew they both carried secret lockets from each other in their wallets, and I didn't want them to be stolen. After another one of those raised-eyebrow looks between them, my mother hid her wallet in the zippered side of her carry-on suitcase. My father placed his in his computer bag, locked both bags and slipped the keys into his pocket. My mother stuck a few dollars in her pocket to spend in the store. I was unaware of it at the time, but they had begun to take some things I said to heart, especially if it sounded like a warning. Once we left the train, my father said, "You two go ahead. I'll stay here by the train." We watched as the older gentleman locked the railroad car door after everyone had left. The cool and refreshing air was a welcome relief after the stale air of the railroad car. I walked with my mother into the store, trying to think of something besides my dream. My mother kept an unusually firm grip on my hand.

Just as everyone walked out of the general store, two gunshots rang out above our heads. I found out later that the older gentleman had told my father where emergency rifles were located underneath the bed of the railroad car and to be ready to use them if necessary. It was definitely necessary. There must have been trouble in this town during previous trips. For just a minute, I thought about the stagecoach robberies in the old Western movies. But we weren't watching a

movie. This was my dream happening in real life. I couldn't remember all of it, but as each moment passed, I realized I had also dreamed that part.

My father and the older gentleman quickly grabbed the guns and positioned themselves between the passengers and the bandits. They reacted so quickly that the bandits stopped short when they realized two long rifles were pointed at them. So far, things were happening just as they had in my dream. Oh, why hadn't I said something earlier?

The older gentleman instructed the passengers to quickly get back on board the railroad car. My mother gripped my hand even more tightly as we hurried onto the train. She and I got to our seats quickly. As the rest of the passengers boarded the railroad car, the bandits were held at bay by my father and the older gentleman. My father then got on board and opened a window so he could keep his rifle aimed at the bandits. Once the older gentleman boarded and joined him at the window, the train began to move. The bandits seemed paralyzed as they stared at the two rifles pointing toward them.

As the general store faded from view, my father handed his rifle to the older gentleman and sat down in the seat next to me across the table from my mother. I thought he looked a little pale as he put his arm around me and reached across the table for my mother's hand.

Suddenly a passenger who was sitting behind us produced a pistol and demanded that my parents give him their wallets. He had obviously watched them being hidden and locked away. I thought, "Oh no! This was in the dream too!" I kept telling myself not to be scared, that maybe things might turn out differently from the dream. Why hadn't I told my parents about my dream? Why hadn't I told them we were going to be in danger of getting robbed? Now if we were shot, it would be my fault because I hadn't told them about my dream. But how could I have known that what happened in the dream would actually happen in real life? I wondered if we would all die on the train. I wondered if I could just disappear into the seat. I just couldn't seem to remember the ending of my dream.

Another thought occurred to me. If I had the ability to dream what was going to happen in the future, why couldn't I do something to change the outcome when it happened in real life, especially if it meant our lives would be saved? An additional dilemma crept into my head. What if changing the outcome in real life would mean I might never have dreams of the future again? Part of me thought about that possibility, and the other part concentrated on trying to remember how the dream ended.

Before I was able to remember any more of the dream, a woman passenger sitting behind the man pointing the gun at my parents hit him hard on the side of his head with her shoe. In the instant of his distraction, my father took his gun away from him. How could the man with the pistol have thought he could carry out a successful robbery and escape the train in broad daylight? I decided that he was an amateur who thought he could intimidate us into submission with his gun. Fortunately for us, he wasn't smart enough to think beyond getting his hands on some money. He let his gun do the talking, and when the gun was removed, he didn't have much to say. After checking to be sure the man had been safely disarmed of all weapons, the older gentleman handcuffed his hands behind his back and locked the cuffs onto a bar at the rear of the railroad car. That would-be robber wasn't going anywhere.

The whole scenario reminded me of playing a previously rehearsed part in a play. I suddenly let out a big sigh. I must have been holding my breath since getting back on the train. I then closed my eyes and was only partially aware that I was mouthing the words of the older gentleman as he spoke on the short-wave radio to Canadian law enforcement. When I opened my eyes, my parents were staring at me.

I was only vaguely aware that others didn't know such things ahead of time. The dream before the train trip was vague, and I had difficulty remembering everything about it. I could only remember the events one piece at a time as they were unfolding in real time.

As I recalled this story, I initially wondered if all of those things were merely imagined in my six-year-old mind. But I'm convinced they really did happen. The acting out of the dream I had before the train trip across the Canadian Rockies was like a letter of introduction to my special gift.

Chapter Two
Wedding Music, a Didgeridoo and Dancing

A month or so before my parents and I traveled to Canada for the wedding of my cousin, **Nidra Wallas**, I had another dream. I was only eight years old. It was so vivid that when I awakened I thought it must have already happened. I dreamed the musician who was scheduled to play the piano at Nidra'a wedding got sick and didn't make it to the church. In the dream, I convinced my parents I could play the piano piece. So along with my parents, I performed the song and dance of eternal love.

After having the dream, I taught myself to play the piano piece just in case the events in the dream came true. Remember, I was only eight years old at the time, but I couldn't help wondering if this dream would prove that I possessed some special abilities.

The church where my cousin was getting married fascinated me. The outside was framed in dull white clapboard, and the inside was painted in off-white colors. My first visit to this church was for the dress rehearsal the evening

before the day of the wedding. My mother said, "War-ne-la, sit here in the third pew where we'll all be sitting during the wedding tomorrow, and tell us if everything seems okay." Both of my parents had a way of making me feel that my comments and opinions were worthy of their consideration. All I had to do was watch everyone practice their parts. The aroma of the freshly cut flowers was beginning to waft through the church, tickling my nose. By tomorrow, I thought, all the buds will be open and the whole church will smell like a flower garden. The wooden benches, hand-hewn a long time ago, had weathered and smoothed out over the years. When I sat down, I could hear the bench practically sing. It must have retained some of the singing energy of previous visitors to the church. The windows of the church were clear glass except for one at the front. It was circular with stained-glass figures of a baby and a man and a woman wearing robes. Hanging underneath the stained-glass window was a plain wooden cross.

I wasn't able to stop staring at the stained-glass window and the cross. I hadn't been inside very many churches, at least that I could remember. The contrast of the colorful, intricate figures in the stained-glass window with the simple wooden cross held my attention. My eyes darted rapidly from the figures in the colorful window to the wooden cross, and the two images fused together for a moment before separating again. I remembered that the cross represented the Christian religion, but I didn't know how Nidra fit into the congregation. I learned later that she wasn't a member at all. It was **Victor MacKenzie**, the man she was about to marry, who was a member of the congregation. I wondered how a couple could decide in whose house of worship a wedding ceremony would take place if they came from different religious or spiritual backgrounds.

The next day, we arrived at the church early. My father was to play his native Australian didgeridoo, and my mother was to perform her native Kwakiutl Indian dance. The musician who normally accompanied them on the piano had flown with us to Vancouver, British Columbia, in the southwestern part of Canada. The pastor met us at the church door with a worried look on his face. He said, "I just received a call from the musician. He's ill and has asked me to tell you that he won't be able to play for the wedding today." As my parents looked at each other in slight bewilderment, I stopped twirling about in my green velvet dress and said, "I can play the piano part." I can still remember their mixed looks of curiosity. Their first look asked, "Is she teasing us?" followed by their look of, "Why do we always act surprised when she says things like this?" I was just learning to recognize that last look.

My father raised his eyebrows and asked, "Do you know this piece?" I answered, "Yes, I taught myself to play it while you were both at work." The piano player and my parents had perfected this unusual piece over the years as a unique combination of their native traditions. I had heard the three of them practicing it many times at our house. My fingers couldn't quite reach all eight keys of an octave; however, I discovered I could hold the tone of the first key by putting my foot on one of the pedals at the bottom of our piano. If I quickly moved my fingers to the second key, it sounded almost as though the two keys had been struck at the same time. I listened to how each of the three pedals changed the tones when I held them down while I tried different piano keys.

"I saw a piano downstairs," I said. "We can go down there, and you can listen to me play the piece." To my slight surprise they agreed, and we all hurried down the steps as the pastor stared after us, his mouth slightly agape.

I shouldn't have been surprised when my parents agreed to follow me downstairs. They often appeared startled or surprised at something I said. One of them would say, "You were right, War-ne-la. How do you know about that?" My usual response was, "I don't know; I just do."

In a far corner of the church basement, I rolled the stool away from the piano. Standing was the only way I could reach the keys with my hands and the bottom pedals with my foot. Before my parents reached the piano, I was already playing the wedding number as softly as I could, hoping the sound wouldn't carry upstairs to the arriving guests.

Once my parents were satisfied that I really could play the piece well enough to accompany my father on the didgeridoo, we climbed the stairs and rejoined the wedding. My father spoke briefly with the pastor, and we entered the sanctuary of the church. My mother walked in front of us, holding onto the arm of an usher, and my father held my hand as we walked behind them all the way down the aisle to the third pew.

When the time came for our musical number, my mother walked toward the front and up the three steps. I followed her, and my father followed behind us. He moved the piano bench to the side, touched my shoulder lightly and murmured, "Are you ready?" I nodded. My mother gave me an encouraging smile and a wink with her left eye, and I responded with a wink from my left eye, a communication that she and I shared. When we both winked, that meant everything was okay. My father was dressed in a dark suit with a royal blue cummerbund around his waist, a matching scarf in his suit pocket and a matching bow tie. He removed the polished dark red didgeridoo from its stand and stood it on the floor, sliding the top part toward him. I was on the other side of the platform standing at the keyboard. My mother, dressed in a smart-looking native dress of red earth tones, was ready to dance between us. With the three of us wearing blue, red and green, it almost seemed like Christmas. The bridal party moved down the steps and to the sides so all of the wedding guests could have a clear view of the dancing against the background of the stained-glass window and the cross. With a nod from my father, the song and dance of eternal love began. My mother had been dancing her whole life. I loved watching her sway to the music as she moved her hands to demonstrate the symbolism of the dance. My father had taken up the didgeridoo at the age of eighteen, when he found out his Australian parentage included some native Aborigine.

The musical performance was quite successful. My memory of the song seemed to be guiding my fingers. A part of me was almost detached from the music I was playing. Another part of me had to concentrate fiercely to be sure I placed my fingers on the piano keys correctly. I'm not sure I breathed during the whole performance, being so intent on getting through the number correctly and living up to the faith my parents had placed in me. I remember reaching a bit late for a few notes. My parents were masters at making the best of any situation, and they were their usual composed selves during the whole number. You might have thought we had been performing together forever, or so it seemed to me. To this day, I hear that wedding piece playing in my head every time I enter a place of worship.

The dance symbolized a combination of creation, love and life. The joining together of the new couple was symbolized by an intricate dance of the hands. It was called a circle dance, which gave thanks to the creator for the sacred things put on the earth for us to use, always in good health. Women were symbolic of Mother Earth, who gave life and nourishment. Men were symbolic of the universe, and, together with the power of the earth, life began.

As my mother danced, her beautiful brown hands moved in the air, and by intertwining her fingers, she communicated the symbolism of two people coming together. She didn't have the long, narrow fingers of a Thai dancer, but they were as long as necessary. Some of my fondest childhood memories were guessing what she was communicating with her hands. When our musical number was finished, I looked up at the wedding party. Nidra was smiling at all three of us. Seeing her reaction made me feel like I had been guided to participate in something really important in our lives. I may have just been living out another dream, but at least this was a good one that came true.

Nidra and I kidded each other for years afterwards about both of us holding our breath while I played the piano for her wedding before I was tall enough to reach the pedals. After the wedding ceremony, I went out to play with the other children. I wanted to get away from the grownups jabbering about my talent and how they were sure that at any minute I was about to erupt into another little Mozart prodigy. I could read my parents' faces pretty well and could see the pride in their eyes.

Looking back on it, I'm sure Nidra's wedding day served as confirmation that I had indeed been given an unusual and special gift. At the tender age of eight, I was filled with so many questions. Could I really have been so sure that my dream about the wedding would come true? Was it because my dream several years before about the train robbery had also played out in real life? Could the dream about the wedding mean that all of my dreams would now come true? Was it possible that the earlier dream about the train robbery set the stage for the dreams and premonitions I experienced throughout my childhood?

War-ne-la's family on her mother's side:

Lamond Wallas *(Chief and flute player)*

– married – **Wanda Dillon** *(drummer and chanter)*

    [War-ne-la's maternal great-grandparents]

    their son: **Fallon Wallas** *(Chief) – married –* **Hannah Hunter**

        [War-ne-la's maternal grandparents]

        their first son: **Mulligan "Wolf" Wallas** *[War-ne-la's uncle]*

          – married – **Galena Grant**

        their second son: **Takus "Deer" Wallas** *[War-ne-la's uncle]*

          – married – **Katia Williams**

        Fallon's daughter: **Kathy "Eagle" Wallas**

          – married – **Dominic Medici**

        their daughter: **War-ne-la Medici**

          Mulligan & Galena's daughter: **Nidra Wallas**

        [War-ne-la's cousin] – married – **Victor MacKenzie** *–*

        {bridal couple in Chapter Two}

          Takus and Katia's son: **Max "Killer Whale" Wallas**

        [War-ne-la's cousin] – married – **Charlene Bering**

Chapter Three
The Music and Energy in our Rock Creek House

Back home in Washington, D.C., after the wedding, my mother inquired of me, "Can you show us what else you've learned to play on the piano?" I played some of the songs I had taught myself. A discussion followed between my parents and me about whether I should take formal lessons. I didn't want to sit through piano lessons because I thought I would be totally bored and felt lessons would keep me from learning on my own. I was barely aware that I was kicking the piano bench while they talked. After a few minutes, they let the subject drop.

As it happened, the musician who had become sick the day of the wedding began to stop by a little more often, and we played the piano together. That was how my parents convinced me to take what passed for formal lessons. I thought I had avoided doing something boring, but in the end, I took the lessons anyway. They just changed the format a little and made it seem like fun for me. I only came to realize later how clever they had been in encouraging my musical talents. I've always been grateful for their persistence.

Music had always been a large part of our lives. It was always playing in the house or in the car. We attended lots of concerts near our home and during our travels. I learned that music was a universal means of communication, no matter where it was playing. My piano teacher helped me appreciate and hear aspects of music that I might never have understood otherwise, such as hearing and playing one melody within another melody. He also taught me how to read music. I could play most music after hearing it, known as "playing by ear," but my piano teacher helped me learn what the quarter, half and full notes meant. He also taught me how to remember to play the flats and sharps and how to keep rhythm in half, three-quarter and four-four time. We practiced the scales every time we got together. Before long, I could play by reading the notes or "by ear" with equal comfort.

Perhaps I had inherited some of my parents' musical talents. My parents often reminded me, "What is important in life is not what we're born with, but how we develop our talents." What I didn't know was how the unusual talents of all the previous generations were developing within my being to set the course of my life. I was continually amazed throughout my childhood every time I learned about the talents of my family members, from intellectual to musical to extrasensory perception (ESP). Apparently my genes incorporated many of their abilities, seen and unseen.

We lived in a three-story house overlooking Rock Creek Park in Washington, D.C. The floor-to-ceiling upper windows made it feel like we lived in the woods. My parents had spent so much of their lives outdoors that they said they chose the house because it made them feel at home. I understood how my mother felt at home looking out at the woods because the area where she grew up in western Canada is filled with huge trees. I often heard her say, "I'm at home here, just like in Canada."

However, my father's country of Australia had mostly short, scrawny trees, not tall ones like in North America. Trees can't grow very tall if they don't get much rain, and sometimes there will be no rain for ten years in the desert of Australia. In the Daintree Rainforest in the northeastern part of Australia, the trees grow larger. During one of our trips to Australia, we took a bus tour of that rainforest. You could hear the obvious pride of the tour guide when he announced, "Australia is one of the few countries in the world that does not allow any cutting of its rainforest." I remember being surprised that palm trees were swaying in the breezes along the eastern coastline. I had to remind myself that Australia really is a South Pacific island—a very large South Pacific island.

My parents each had a study overlooking the back woods running down to Rock Creek, which they said gave them inspiration for their work, even when it was dark. Their routine was to put in an hour or two of work at their desks and home computers nearly every evening after my bedtime. My room was between their two studies. They took turns looking in on me. When I heard footsteps, I would quickly turn out the flashlight I used to read under the covers and would pretend to be sleeping. That usually went on for several hours before I fell asleep. I had so much energy and my thoughts ran so wild in my head that it was hard for me to settle down to sleep. Because there was so much to read and learn, I didn't want to waste any time with unnecessary sleeping.

It must have been a surprise when I was born. My parents married as they were turning forty and probably assumed they would never have children. Given their unusual cultural backgrounds, it shouldn't have been such a surprise that I was a little different from other children. Incorporating their two separate cultures as well as my childcare provider's culture, plus trying to be a regular American girl, created many disconnects and conflicts during my childhood.

Because of my dark skin, contrasting blue eyes and what I thought of as unusual facial features, I sometimes felt like a bit of a social misfit. I didn't fit into any particular school clique and sometimes felt shunned by the more popular girls in my school. I was a good student, and because I had been reading since I was five, I often knew the answers to the questions the teacher asked before the rest of the class. In fact, I usually knew what questions the teacher planned to ask, but I made sure I didn't share that information with any of my classmates. The combination made me feel lonely at times. Once in grade school, two bouncy blonde girls threatened me during gym class to stop being a "smarty-pants" in class or they would find a pair of scissors to cut my long curly hair. I realized that any abilities I had been given to help me understand the future weren't much help in making me feel better about myself when the girls were mean to me. Whenever I was troubled by something, my favorite refuge was to bury myself in a book. Once the book was opened, my world immediately changed.

Home was an entirely different atmosphere from school. We had a busy and stimulating household. When I was well-behaved, my parents referred to me as their million-dollar child. I didn't know if that meant there had been only a one-in-a-million chance that I might have been born or that they wouldn't trade me for a million dollars. That illusion gave way to reality pretty quickly. When my behavior left something to be desired, one of them would tease me, "I was offered three cents for you today, and I'm seriously considering the offer!" It didn't take much to keep me in line and keep any "only child" behavior to a minimum.

They didn't know about my imaginary, rich fantasy life when the real War-ne-la came to life. I didn't have to be the obedient child for my parents during those times. In my fantasy life I could be anything or anyone I wanted to be. However, the powers I held in my fantasy life paled in comparison to my dreams. I traveled to so many exciting and frequently scary worlds in my dreams that sometimes when I woke up I wasn't sure which reality I was in—the current one of my daily life, my imagined fantasy life, or a dream. Things always happened fast in all three of my worlds.

When I tried to carry any of my imaginary fantasy powers over into my real life, my parents presented a united front when it came to reminding me who held the real power in the household. There were plenty of reminders of who was in charge, whether it was my choice of clothing or occasional misbehavior. I can still hear my mother saying, "What message do you think those clothes you're wearing will give to the rest of your classmates?" And if my behavior wasn't appropriate, my father would ask, "Is that how you would behave if we were at the White House?" Their comments put the responsibility for my behavior right where it belonged: within me. The lesson about taking responsibility for my behavior had to be repeated more often than I might like to remember.

War-ne-la's family on her father's side:

Emelio Medici – *married* – **Gina Orzo** *{Italians}*
> *[War-ne-la's paternal grandparents]*
> *– (both migrated from Italy to Australia after World War II)*

their son: **Dominic Medici** – *married* – **Kathy "Eagle" Wallas** –
> *(British Columbian Kwakiutl)*

their daughter: **War-ne-la Medici**

Chapter Four
Ancestral Connection to Namesake

In a book at our home, there is a picture taken in 1914 of my shaman namesake, **War-ne-la**. She was a famous shaman from my mother's Kwakiutl [Kwa ' kee ' yoo'tl] tribe of British Columbia in the southwestern part of Canada.

[The Kwakiutls have revised the spelling of their name to: *Kwakwaka'wakw*].

I gazed into her lean, intelligent face and saw her high cheekbones, but I couldn't tell from looking at the photograph what color her eyes were. She had such an all-knowing look about her, not unlike Leonardo da Vinci's painting of *Mona Lisa*. Her presence seemed almost real to me. I could actually feel her looking at me. Would I look like her as I got older?

From what I could remember about my pre-school years, I seemed to know what was going to happen ahead of time and what conversation was going to take place. I didn't know how I knew. It may have come from my dreams or daydreams. Or it may have come from deep within my brain. I could have practically repeated the conversation right along with the person speaking during the actual happening.

So I figured out from the time I started school that since my parents had named me after a shaman, they must have had some premonition or idea of what I might be able to see or know. I was never sure how much they expected of me or what things I did or said might surprise them. I would occasionally overhear one of my parents asking the other, "What's our little shaman been up to today?"

My mother was a professor in the Department of Psychology at the American University, located in Washington, D.C. She taught psychology classes all over the world. Her specialty was counseling indigenous, or native, populations. That's how she happened to meet my father. He was taking a few graduate courses in Australia when he decided to attend my mother's two-day class. He told one of our neighbors, "I often looked for ways to better understand my Aboriginal heritage, and enrolling in Professor Wallas' course was part of my fieldwork. I had no idea at the time how that one decision would change my life forever. I found the love of my life, and it provided my introduction to North America."

After the course ended, a correspondence between my parents began immediately. Many times I heard them tell people, "We both fell in love at first sight." Their courtship took place across several oceans while he finished his master's degree.

After my parents married and my mother became Kathy Medici, they moved to Washington, D.C. Kathy wasn't her real name, of course. Her real name was a native, almost unpronounceable Kwakiutl name, with only five letters, but with four syllables within those five letters —K w ik w—meaning *eagle*. Her maiden name was Wallas, and she believed she was a descendant of James Wallas, the hereditary chief of the Quatsino Band of the Northern Vancouver Island Kwakiutls. The Kwakiutl spelling of Wallas was W' ales (with the 'e' upside down).

My mother was the more outgoing conversationalist in the family. She had two voices: one rather soft that she used normally and the other a louder lecturing voice that she used in her classrooms. Her unusual background as a Native American, known as *First Nations* in Canada, elicited a certain amount of curiosity from others. After relating an abbreviated version of her life, she would quickly draw others out. Before long, they would be talking up a storm about themselves. She often cranked those real-life stories into her teaching. Along with the stories of their visible lives, I loved the way she was able to weave their inner, or spiritual, lives into so many of her lectures. She was able to hear and understand both parts of their lives. I think that may have been a particular talent of hers, because she accomplished it so effortlessly. Observing her talent may have been how I became so comfortable with the spiritual side of life early on.

After being in a classroom with her, she would ask me, "Did you hear anything in this class that you hadn't heard before?" She was almost as good as my father at getting me to tell her what I had observed or heard in her classroom, which then led to questions like, "I didn't understand the question asked about the Ainu of Japan and how they became a minority in their own country." My mother would say, "Do you remember what I told you about the Mayan people of Central America and how their culture came close to extinction when the Spaniards invaded their land?" Then we would see how many cultures I could recall that had been virtually extinguished throughout the world once others took over their land. When we finished the review of the classroom questions and answers, she would say, "What do you think was going on in the mind of the person who asked about the Ainu?" Then we got into the spiritual side of people. My mother helped me learn how to distinguish between the spoken question and what the student was really trying to find out. I learned that body language and the tone of voice was often more revealing than the spoken word. Often the conversation continued all the way home. Sometimes I wondered if she kept both of us talking so she could stay awake during the drive.

My father was an occasional guest professor at Georgetown University's International Peace Program. He was a natural choice as a lecturer, since he worked for the Department of Agriculture and traveled all over the world in that capacity. His job was to work for peace through agriculture. When anyone asked about the connection between peace and agriculture, he countered with the question, "What could represent working for peace more effectively than ending starvation in the world? If everyone is well-fed and there's no worry about where their next meal is coming from, won't they be more interested in pursuits other than fighting?" His practical background of growing grapes in the Australian family vineyards provided an unusual entry into the field. His educational background of agronomy, biology, and marketing, and his Australian accent, were an added plus. He had a ready smile and an ability to put people instantly at ease.

I've watched my father address groups of farmers from different countries. Usually, the farmers were angry about their inability to compete in the global market because the Congress of the United States appropriated money to subsidize, or pay for, many crops grown by American farmers. My father opened the meetings with a statement, "Everyone's concerns will be given an adequate hearing." With that opening, he managed to calm the farmers down and then facilitated a spirited discussion on the issue. He once said to me, "You know, most people just want someone to listen to them." He didn't adjourn a meeting until the last person standing in line to speak had been given an opportunity to be heard. He was a master at commanding respect from others. After each meeting he would say to me, "So, did you learn anything new?" More than anyone else in my life, my father encouraged me to express myself articulately. He was teaching me the art of debating, but I didn't realize it at the time. He taught me how to make my point clearly without alienating other participants in a discussion and how to respectfully stay on point until I was sure everyone understood my viewpoint. We have continued that practice, and he has remained my favorite debating partner all of my life.

Chapter Five
Adoptive African Family

During the times I didn't travel with my parents, our nanny, **Uli Batta Zendra**, took care of me. My parents met Uli and her daughter, **Kilmer,** during one of their trips to Africa while my mother was pregnant with me. UIi, with her young daughter Kilmer in tow, was fleeing from a forced marriage to an old man after Uli's husband, **Keon Zendra**, had died. She would have become the old man's fourth wife.

Uli and Kilmer had hitched rides and walked from the desert of northern Mali for four days and nights to Bamako, the capital city where the university is located. Uli knew some English and sought out my parents when she saw them arrive at the university. My parents listened to their plight and agreed to bring the two of them back to America. Uli's arrival in America solved the child-care problems my parents would have faced once I was born. The immigration office classified her as a child-care provider. I wondered if the immigration agents looked the other way as Kilmer hid behind her mother's long dress upon their arrival. That may not be how it happened, but when I first heard the story, I had a visual image of Kilmer trying to make herself invisible inside the folds of Uli's flowing African dress. From the moment of their arrival in America, our lives were intertwined. Uli and Kilmer became as much a part of our family as anyone possibly could have.

Apparently my father had been absolutely taken with Kilmer's dark, flashing eyes. Sometimes when she was out of sorts, he would start singing the Johnny Mercer lyrics, "Jeepers Creepers, Where'd You Get Those Peepers? Jeepers, Creepers, Where'd You Get Those Eyes?" He could always get her laughing and her eyes flashing again in a few minutes. As long as I could remember, my father gave both of us lots of attention. He seemed to provide a father figure for Kilmer. Since Kilmer didn't remember her own father, I thought she was fortunate that my father took such an active interest in her. My father and Kilmer both loved watching old American musicals, and they were always singing the songs from those movies around the house and yard.

Our Australian shepherd dog, *Aussie*, our calico cat, *Cascade*, Kilmer and I roamed beyond the back yard to the woods of Rock Creek, pretending we were trekking across the Great Outback, or interior, of Australia. That would have been an unlikely prospect, since the Great Outback of Australia is mostly a desert. Other times we pretended to be running through the woods and across

the fields of British Columbia or across the plains of Africa. I was always on some journey in my imagination and dreams. Aussie and Cascade, Kilmer and I understood each other perfectly. We seemed to know what each was thinking. When running through the woods, I sometimes felt as though Kilmer and I were running as fast as the animals and that the four of us comprised one pack. It was through our kinship with Uli and Kilmer that my family learned about the continent of Africa. Tribal wars in Africa were frequent news topics, and I frequently dreamed about the turmoil. I talked to Uli about my African dreams and learned that we often experienced the same dreams. Uli always provided comfort for me after my scary dreams. She's tall, and I can still remember the comforting embrace of her long arms reaching down to hug me whenever I shared my nighttime horrors.

I've watched Uli stand and rock back and forth from heel to toe when she was worried about something. I always knew something terrible had happened when I saw her in that rocking mode. Her eyes seemed to be focused on something a million miles away. A low-volume, high-pitched sound came out of her mouth when she was rocking back and forth. I learned not to say anything to her during those times. Through our reading and watching international news stories on the television, we usually discovered whatever it was that had caused Uli to start rocking. She worried about her family and only rarely got any direct news about them. It would take a trip to Africa for Uli and Kilmer to reunite with the surviving members of her family. I was able to accompany them on that trip the summer after Kilmer graduated from college. As I came to realize, Uli was also "one who knows."

One of my special early memories was when my father, Kilmer and I read. He let us climb onto the couch with him while he read a book to us. When

Kilmer learned how to read, the two of them took turns reading. Between the children's educational television shows, plus Kilmer always around to read to me, I learned how to read before I started kindergarten. When I learned how, we all shared the reading.

Uli and Kilmer lived in an apartment over our garage. Uli stayed busy with her education, which my parents helped her obtain. She has been earning college credits for as long as I can remember. She did substitute teaching when she could spare the time and when she wasn't taking care of me and her daughter. It helped her earn some extra money. Uli and Kilmer were invited to have dinner with us at any time, and they often delighted us with their presence.

I could listen to Uli's accent forever. Her voice had a clipped English-accented lilt and a deep, throaty African sound, both at the same time. She didn't speak until she was sure she had all verb tenses correct and was using the correct meaning for her words. Sometimes it delayed her response in conversation, but the wait was worth it. I understood later that hers and everyone's personal experience with the collective unconscious, the inherited knowledge of our evolution, bounded across the millennia. Uli and Kilmer represented a living, breathing bridge to the beginning of civilization. My mother, father and I all agreed that Uli and Kilmer were the best thing that ever happened to us. I hope in some small way the reverse was true for them, but if not, that's okay too.

Kilmer was two years older than I, but we played together all the time when we were little. The more time we spent together, the better we could read each other, almost like a book. But we did have our share of quarrels during our childhood. She once tore the ribbon off my new Easter hat. My mother quickly figured out the problem and thereafter doubled her purchases. She would arrive home with two of something, and say, "I couldn't decide which one to buy, so I got both and now each of you can wear one." She would have us take turns getting first choice. Sometimes she varied her presentation by saying, "The store was offering two for the price of one, so each of you can have one." My mother was respectful in the way she presented gifts to Uli and Kilmer. I often tried to emulate her graciousness.

If Kilmer ever felt more disadvantaged than I, she never told me. She had a lot of energy and wasn't shy about expressing her opinions. The neighborhood boys teased us, unmercifully at times, because of our dark skin and the color of my eyes. We were known as "Black" and "Blue." The more they teased us, the closer we held onto each other. Out of necessity, we looked out for one another. I once overheard one of the boys call Kilmer a "black-eyed spear chucker" and me a "blue-eyed witch doctor." Kilmer took after him and chased him through the woods of Rock Creek. I never knew anyone who could run as lightning-fast as Kilmer. That boy didn't have a prayer of outrunning her, as he soon discovered. Kilmer wouldn't tell me what happened, but he never called us those names again. Despite our childhood quarrels and the separate paths our lives took, Kilmer has remained my best friend throughout my life.

When Uli was a young girl, someone gave her the poem, *Trees*, by Joyce Kilmer. Uli's home in the northern part of Mali was a desert with no trees, so she could only imagine what trees looked like. She dreamed of seeing a real tree someday. That's why she loved that poem and why she named her daughter after its author. She wanted a constant reminder of her dream. Uli was an adult before she saw a real tree. If that one dream of seeing a real tree came true, perhaps other dreams would also come true. Kilmer was completely "Americanized" but fiercely protective of her mother. I loved that about her. They were their own cocooned unit of self-preservation and self-protection. When my parents were gone, the two of them spent the night in our guest room. Aussie was our watch dog, and Cascade was supposed to be our attack cat, when she wasn't sleeping, that is. I didn't realize at the time how fortunate I was to have so many different cultures swirling around me. That exposure would help me a great deal later in my life when I began traveling the world.

Uli had masks from all over Africa hanging on the wall of their living room. It took some concentration, but I eventually came to see the masks as friendly spirits. She could keep my hair standing on end with some of the stories about her native Africa. She would hide behind one of her African masks and change her voice so she sounded like the person in the mask and would pretend to fight off a cheetah or some other wild animal. She would also make the animal sounds from behind the mask. Each story was different. It was always a relief to see her come out from behind the mask and be herself again. I wondered if she made up the stories as she went along, but the few times I checked the authenticity of her stories at the library, her recitations of native lore were true.

The legend behind one of the masks came to life during my pre-adolescence. The mask was blue and round, almost the way the earth appears from outer space. Uli said its spirit protected people from the dangers of storms while at sea. I stared at that mask for a long time every time I visited them. After awhile the spirit began talking to me about what was going on in my life. Uli said, "When nothing else can protect someone from drowning, the spirit behind the blue mask comes to the rescue." The spirit behind the blue mask kept telling me we would meet again in another place.

Kilmer turned into quite a showman with her natural dancing abilities. She danced to African music most of the time. I came to realize that the music she and I loved so much began in Africa. I tried several times to accompany her dancing with my piano playing, but I couldn't play fast enough for her moves. She entered dancing contests in the area and frequently won first prize. No matter how hard I tried to learn how to dance, I just couldn't keep up with her moves. That special talent of hers would help her decide the course of her life's work. As it happened, we went off in totally separate directions after we grew up. She never lost her interest in dancing, and I never lost my interest in playing the piano.

In a corner of our back yard was a huge rock, left behind from the glaciers melting after the last Ice Age. We called it our meditation rock. One clear summer day, Kilmer was lying in the grass next to the rock. As I was about to sit on it, a perfectly intact snakeskin began coming out from under the rock. Kilmer and I watched in fascination as the snakeskin continued to materialize, almost as though it were coming from the rock itself. When the formation of the snakeskin stopped, I took the fully formed snakeskin and wrapped it around the "hand of fate" which was really a fallen tree limb, as a reminder of the continuity of life, no matter in what form. It was well into summer before I once again felt comfortable sitting on that meditation rock, and then only after a careful look all around to be certain there were no surprises waiting for me. Finding the snakeskin represented one more omen of the sacred powers I was about to acquire for my life's work. Now I had my very own "rainbow serpent" common in Australian Aboriginal mythology. Could the rainbow serpent be one of my totems, an emblem of my ancestry?

It was not unusual for Kilmer and me to beat our drums and shake our rattles as we chanted and whooped our way through the woods of Rock Creek. I often danced with the animal spirits as we all ran along the creek.

Sometimes I had the strange feeling that I had become one of them. The neighborhood children occasionally joined our impromptu gatherings. The older boys watched from the top of the hill most of the time, but only joined in if they happened to be right there when we started our rattling and drumming and dancing.

It was a healthy outlet for our energy, and I wondered if any of the other children felt the presence of the animal spirits as I did. Even the spiders and snakes became a part of me. The medicine men or shamans of Aboriginal Australia had special relationships with the rainbow serpent and its powers. During the acting out of our native customs, there were times when I felt I was looking at a desert mirage as my Aboriginal ancestors once did. Other times I imagined being in a circle ceremony, drumming and dancing with my Kwakiutl ancestors to the call of the spirits. In Navajo mythology, the spider represents the figure of a grandmother. Even though I'm not Navajo, I wondered if I could have been "dancing" or imitating the spirit of my grandmothers and my shaman ancestors.

It was probably natural that we would all try different dances to accompany our rattling and drumming. Being the least capable dancer, I usually volunteered to be the drummer while the others danced, joining the dancing only when I felt moved by the spirits to do so. Drumming and dancing aren't mutually exclusive, and I discovered I could do both. It felt good to get into the rhythm. Kilmer taught the neighborhood kids some of the African dances she had learned from her mother. She probably didn't know it at the time, but she was setting in place her life-long passion of teaching dance to children. When our parents came out on the porch and joined us with our drumming, Kilmer yelled, "Are we all in touch or what?"

Jimalee Burton of the Cherokee nation said about drums, "From the beginning there were drums, beating out world rhythm – the booming, never-failing tide on the beach; the four seasons, gliding smoothly, one from the other; when the birds come, when they go, the bear hibernating for his winter sleep. Unfathomable the why, yet all in perfect time. Watch the heartbeat in your wrist —a precise pulsing beat of life's Drum—with loss of timing you are ill."

Hardly a day goes by that I don't beat my drum, even if only for a few minutes. It keeps me in touch with Mother Earth.

War-ne-la's Adoptive Family:

Keon Zendra – *married* – **Uli Batta** *(both born and married in Africa)*

their daughter: **Kilmer Zendra** – *(born in Africa)*

{Uli and Kilmer Zendra migrated from Africa to the

U.S.A. after Keon's death, when Kilmer was two years old}

Chapter Six
Papa's Italian and Australian Aborigine Birthright

My father's parents, **Emilio Medici** and **Gina Orzo**, had traveled to Australia from the southern part of their native Italy after World War II. They were all dark-skinned, so everyone assumed their Mediterranean heritage had kept their skin dark. It may have been true for my grandparents, but as we were to learn, my father wasn't Italian at all.

His mother died when he was eighteen, and at that time his father told him she was part Aborigine. She wasn't, but apparently my grandfather couldn't bring himself to tell his son the whole truth about his background. My father said, "After my mother's death, I began to understand why I always felt the natives looked at me a little differently and our interactions felt so natural. Somewhere bouncing around in the back of my head was the thought that we shared a special bond. They were able to see something in me that I couldn't see during my childhood. That may have been the reason why I've been so comfortable with the Aborigines of my country." As we learned later, that was only part of the story.

It was after his mother's death that my father began playing the didgeridoo. He said, "Playing the didgeridoo came easily, and it felt like the right thing to do." I figured he was trying to recapture some of his heritage. He was obviously proud of his Aboriginal blood because he mentioned it whenever anyone asked him about his accent or where he was from.

We had at least six didgeridoos in our basement, mounted on stands. My father played them periodically to keep them in good working order. I could listen to him play them forever. I didn't realize that he was instilling in me a love for his native music. Sometimes I danced while my father played or when I listened to one of David Hudson's compact discs. I always felt close to nature when I heard the playing of a didgeridoo.

When I was ten, my father began teaching me how to play the didgeridoo. Playing takes tremendous breath control and a lot of hard work. To make the music, you have to blow into the didgeridoo, similar to a horse blubbering its lips when exhaling. It takes a lot of air to keep that blowing or blubbering going, which means you have to keep replenishing the supply of air. Learning to breathe through my nose and exhale through my mouth at the same time took a lot of practice. I wasn't sure I would ever get the hang of it. My father would say, "Breathe normally for a few minutes, and then try playing again." He showed a lot of patience with me. He assured me that once I mastered the playing I would feel the vibrations deep inside myself, which would then create a feeling of detachment, as if I were actually floating. It turned out he was absolutely right. The more modern flute is probably the closest thing to feeling the wind or pulse of nature, which could be why Native Americans have been playing flutes for so long. When you've learned to play the didgeridoo successfully, you've mastered the art of breath control. I could not have known that learning how to control my breath would save my life a few years later.

(See APPENDIX to Chapter Six in back of book to learn how didgeridoos are created.)

My father shared with others his culture of the didgeridoo and other Aboriginal art. Several times a year he would participate in a teaching camp for people who wanted to learn how to play the didgeridoo. He always let me accompany him to the sessions. Many of the participants were curious about the natives of Australia. Listening to my father answer their questions was another way I learned about our Aboriginal heritage. Each person who attended the camp would be given a computer printout of didgeridoo makers in Australia. Those who were interested in purchasing one could contact the makers themselves.

The rest of our basement was filled with native artworks from all over the world. They weren't for sale, but each piece had a stack of cards next to it. People from everywhere came to visit us, and I would see them carrying several cards in their hands as they left.

I spent time sitting in front of the many dots in Aboriginal art, trying to get inside the artists' heads to understand what story was being told. I learned that the dots in the pictures of the Aborigines reflected the dots in their native lands. The white is like the spinifex, a sharp-edged grass used for building huts and other things. The blue is like the eucalyptus leaves, and the lemon-green is like other tufted grasses that grow all over the Australian desert. After gazing at the pictures for a little while, the animals or people in the pictures jumped off the canvas and revealed the stories of their lives. They "spoke" to me in a language that I understood.

The crocodile is often featured in the aboriginal art. We had a piece that portrayed the legend of a crocodile named Ganhaarr who captured a woman and her baby from the riverbank and took them to his underwater cave below the river bed. According to the legend, she became his wife and he took the child as his own. She lived with him so long that she began laying eggs. Her family tried to locate her, but all they could ever find were her eggs! If the legend had a meaning, it may have been to remind humans that animals could occasionally outsmart them. I loved seeing manifestations of the power of animals, no matter what species or in what artistic format.

My father had always believed that his parents met after his father moved to Australia and that they were married there. That wasn't what happened, as we

were to discover later when going through the family safe after my grandfather's death. My grandparents were married on board the ship that took them to Australia. To me that sounded like the most romantic way possible to begin their new lives together.

My father kept a picture on his desk at home of his parents and him as a small boy standing between them. They looked like the perfect family. From my father's stories of his childhood, I would have agreed that they were. I'm sorry I never got to meet my paternal grandmother Gina. She must have been a strong woman to have gone through World War II and then a move to a different country. They were married for twenty-five years before she died.

From the minute we arrived at my grandfather's house in Melbourne, Australia, I could always sense some kind of tension between him and my father on the subject of my father's Aboriginal heritage. At one point, I overheard my father ask my grandfather, "Why didn't you tell me before she died?" My grandfather answered, "We just didn't think it was that important." The air seemed heavy around the two of them whenever we visited Australia. My father seemed to be lost in his thoughts a lot of the time when my grandfather was around. The strain between them seemed to get worse with each visit. I didn't like what my senses would pick up from my father during our visits, so I tended to make myself scarce whenever he got into his darker moods.

While I valued my father's serious nature, I loved his dry sense of humor.

He was not one to suffer small talk and was known as "a man of few words." But when he did speak, I noticed how everyone listened to what he had to say. He was soft-spoken but very deliberative in his Australian-accented speech. He had a favorite trick he played on people who visited us. My father would be doing a perfectly obvious chore, and yet someone would invariably ask him what he was doing. If washing the car, he would say with that great deadpan expression of his, "I thought it was obvious; I'm milking a cow!" Comments like that spoke volumes about how he valued spending his time productively and how he expected conversation to be meaningful.

My father's family was in the wine business in Australia. They were among the first to realize how perfect the soil conditions in southeastern Australia were for growing grapes. They were carrying on a tradition they had followed back in Italy, before they migrated to Australia. My father had learned the family wine business while working at the vineyard during his adolescence. After he graduated from university, he worked as part of the professional staff. He didn't find the fulfillment he was seeking, however, so he began to respond to his need to broaden his horizons academically and spiritually. That's how he came to enroll in my mother's class of counseling indigenous peoples.

Whenever we traveled to Australia, we visited the family vineyards. I had heard the story of how in Italy they stomped the grapes with their bare feet to squeeze the juice out for making the wine. In Australia they put the grapes into huge vats with electric rotating crushers. The juice from the grapes drained into large containers and was then processed into wine. Whenever I saw the wine-making operation, I couldn't help but wonder what it would feel like to stomp the grapes with bare feet. I once asked, "Grandpapa, is it true they stomped the grapes with their bare feet in Italy?" My grandfather, in his raspy voice, answered, "Yes it is, and someday I would like to experience that sensation again. When you're a little older, I'll take you to Italy and we'll stomp the grapes together." We never made the time to do it, and then it was too late.

The feud, whatever it was between my father and grandfather, went on. The only time it seemed to dissipate was when they cooked together in my grandfather's kitchen, the largest room in his house. My mother and I would set the table and then watch them cook together. It was almost like watching a play.

My grandfather was short and robust with white hair. My father was tall and thin with curly dark hair. When my grandfather cooked, he used everything in the kitchen. By the time he finished, the kitchen looked like it had been ravaged by a wild kangaroo. My father was neat and preferred to wash the dirty dishes and pans right away. He seemed to be constantly trailing my grandfather and cleaning up after him. They barked orders at each other all during the preparations. My father would ask, "How do you expect me to get the pasta and all that sauce into such a small dish?" My grandfather would answer, "You think I'm worried about something as silly as the size of a dish right now?" And my father would answer, "Oh, how ridiculous of me to realize that the sauce in that big pot might not fit into this dish; but that's okay, Papa, you keep cooking while I find a bigger one and that way you won't have to think about the sauce spilling all over the counter when you're taking it out of the pot." Grandfather would say, "That's a good idea; at least you'll be out from under my feet for a few minutes." As my father grumbled and traipsed over to the big cupboards, my grandfather would make huge expansive gestures with his arms, as though trying to take up the space in the kitchen for himself. Sometimes the scenes went on way past what might have been a curtain call in a real play.

When they finally finished the food preparation, they carried their Italian specialties to the table. All the aromas created dizzying sensations. My nose would twitch and my stomach would growl with anticipation. There were at least three different types of pasta, each with a different sauce of seafood, veal, beef or venison. Salads and vegetables added to the colorful mix. As the dishes were set on the table, with little room to spare, a large basket of freshly baked bread would appear in my grandfather's hand. Any remaining stress magically disappeared, as my grandfather again became his loving self and my father returned to his unstressed self.

Once the atmosphere became serene, we all began participating in a fabulous Italian dinner, served with Australian wines from the family vineyards. My grandfather poured wine in our glasses, with one or two teaspoons in mine. As he poured, he would say, "I'm carrying on our family's tradition! I would like to toast my lovely Gina and the rest of our ancestors. I offer thanks to the Heavenly Father for blessing our family with good health and for the opportunity to live in this adopted country of Australia." Then he made the sign of the cross. Once he finished, the feast that equaled no others began. I can recall with almost no effort the smells of the tomatoes, meats, cheeses and the fresh bread. Occasionally when I enter someone's home and smell or see some food that reminds me of those delicious dinners at my grandfather's, I'm momentarily transported back to my grandfather's homey kitchen in Australia. More than once I've found myself unconsciously licking my lips in anticipation of an Italian meal about to be served.

Being around my father and grandfather at the same time helped me understand that emotions between two people could also be felt by a third person. That may have been how I began developing my extrasensory perception (ESP). I often knew what my father and grandfather were thinking. Sometimes I could sense that my father was imagining his ancestors walking across the desert or Great Outback of Australia. My grandfather would be wondering why the Aborigines had never adapted to the white men's ways. The conflicts in their thinking would crash into each other since they came from totally different directions. But it was only in my mind that the crashing would occur, because I was the only one who knew what each of them was thinking. I wasn't completely comfortable knowing what other people were thinking, so I tried to bury those thoughts in my subconscious. Getting comfortable with knowing what others were thinking didn't come until I grew up. As a child, I just assumed everyone else could see and feel the same things I could. Since it came so naturally to me, I didn't think of it as anything special or unusual.

There were many times when I became unsettled and a little bit scared with the information I gleaned from sensing the emotions and thoughts of others. I often had to disappear for awhile to get away from people whose minds I was sensing. I didn't understand all those grown-up ideas and thoughts people had. For a long time I didn't realize that many of my dreams were the result of what got stored in the subconscious part of my brain. No wonder I dreamed of things happening before they actually did. My subconscious was trying to release the information and energy into my conscious reality. During the daytime I didn't allow myself to think about some of the things I sensed, so that information stayed hidden in my brain. Once I fell asleep, I had no control over my subconscious, which gave whatever was in there the freedom to rise to the surface of reality. But a dream isn't reality—or is it? There were times when I wasn't sure.

Chapter Seven
Mama's Kwakiutl Birthright and Totem Poles

My mother was the only daughter of a Kwakiutl tribal chief in British Columbia, Canada. She has two older brothers, **Mulligan and Takus Wallas**, who live in their native world and make their living helping others learn about their heritage. Mulligan owns a boat and takes people sightseeing and fishing in the waters off British Columbia. Takus owns a store and sells native art and accessories, along with supplies for hunting and fishing expeditions.

I learned from my Canadian uncles the story of the musical abilities of their paternal grandparents, my great-grandparents, **Lamond and Wanda Wallas**. My great-grandfather was a Kwakiutl tribal chief, which afforded my great-grandmother, as his wife, a certain prestige. Drumming is a huge, sacred part of tribal culture. I think of drumming as a way of kissing Mother Earth and thanking her for providing all of life's sustenance. I like to think I'm carrying on their traditions. Drumming is also like the heartbeat of Mother Earth, and tribal drumming appears to match the earth's pulse rate. Apparently my great-grandmother was a talented drummer and chanter who knew how to draw the fish toward the shore, making capture by the tribe easier. Whenever game was scarce, my great-grandmother was called upon to perform her hypnotizing drumming and singing. My great-grandfather loved the wooden flute, carved by the members of the tribe. They sometimes performed together to lure the fish.

My maternal grandparents, **Fallon and Hannah Wallas**, were insistent about the importance of getting a good education. Their sons, my uncles, had little interest in school. They preferred to swim, fish and hunt in the wilderness of western Canada. My mother was the bookworm in the family. Every weekend she brought as many books home from the public school library as her small arms could carry. During the summer months, she frequented the public library and borrowed as many as were allowed to be checked out at one time. Sometimes she would finish all of them in a few days and return to the library for another stack. My grandparents were proud of her interest in education. They rarely discouraged her from her reading pleasure.

In Canada, college is attainable for anyone who makes the effort. My mother plowed ahead and whizzed through her formal education. She had always been interested in studying people, so psychology was a natural college major for her. She continued to live at home except for the times her classes were held farther away. My grandparents weren't knowledgeable about the degree process, but they knew my mother must have been doing the right thing. The thirst for knowledge seemed to consume her.

My uncles would say to me, "You're just like your mother when she was a school girl." I think I must have been, except for my blue eyes. I identified with an old Arapaho proverb, "If we wonder often, the gift of knowledge will come." I always had a backpack full of books when we visited the family in Canada during my childhood. I read the books under the covers at night. I made sure I carried a flashlight and several extra packets of batteries whenever I traveled.

During the daytime, my cousins and extended cousins and I sailed the waters and roamed the vast wilderness of British Columbia. That's when I got hands-on learning about the hereditary lands of my mother's tribe. Once while

hiking over the Queen Charlotte Islands, we came upon a decaying totem pole that had fallen over. We sat with it for awhile. I could hear it speaking to me through its tears about the loss of its people during the smallpox epidemic. The totem pole seemed to still have some energy attached, so I imbued myself with some of it by rubbing my hands over its smooth wood. I knew all of its physical matter was in the process of returning to the earth to be reborn as something else at a future time.

Originally, the Kwakiutls lived on the banks of the Queen Charlotte Strait and its inlets. Now, many of them, including my uncles and their families, have moved farther inland. My uncles and their families lived east of Powell River, a small city about 90 miles north of Vancouver. The books in their houses were filled with native poetry and legends. We read them together after supper. My cousins Nidra, Victor, Max, and Charlene kept trying to explain the meaning of the tribal legends to me. Sometimes they called me their "city slicker cousin." I loved the tribe's reverence for all living things portrayed in their poetry.

Kwakiutl Prayer To A Cedar Tree

Look at me, friend!

I have come to ask for your dress,

for you have come to take pity on us;

for there is nothing for which you cannot be used,

because it is your way that there is nothing

for which we cannot use you,

for you are really willing to give us your dress.

I have come to beg you for this,

long-life maker, for I am going to make

a basket for lily roots out of you.

There's a poem about salmon, the staple of the Kwakiutl diet:

When a man eats salmon by the river, he sings the salmon song.

It is in the river

in the roasting

in the spearing

in the sharing

in the shoring

in the shaking shining salmon.

It is in the song too.

While my mother was still in her early twenties, she was granted her Ph.D. degree. After the granting of her doctorate, and with a long farewell to family and friends, she left her safe and secure world in Canada and began her teaching career. She was one of the few professors knowledgeable about indigenous peoples, and it seemed every university in the country wanted to add that class to their graduate psychology program. Thus began my mother's worldly travels. She learned to live out of two suitcases and carry all her teaching materials and portable typewriter in two briefcases. Traveling just about everywhere in the world to learn more about each country's indigenous peoples increased her value as a traveling professor. If my parents had not married, she might not have settled down to one university and he might not have taken a position with the United States government. I heard her tell someone once, "I loved the itinerant way of life, but as I got older, I loved the feel of my own bed and the familiar smell of my own sheets more."

My mother had dark, all-seeing eyes, just like my father. You could tell she was a native of the Americas from a mile away. Her olive skin and thick black hair, often braided, were beautiful. She was shorter than my father, but not by much. She almost always wore native dress, including native jewelry. Dressmakers and jewelers from her home area in Canada asked her to model what they made. They would send her something with a stack of business cards, and if someone expressed interest in purchasing clothes or jewelry similar to what she was wearing, she would hand them a card and ask them to contact the maker directly. That was my mother's way of keeping her heritage alive and helping some members of her Kwakiutl tribe sustain themselves.

In our back yard in Washington, we had a meditation circle with a seating area, flowers, herbs and a "hand of fate." In the middle of that circle was a totem pole from my mother's tribe. The totem pole was created to honor their tribal chief, my grandfather, on his 50th birthday. The pictures of the potlatch, the feast and celebration raising the totem pole honoring my grandfather, fascinated me. I looked at the album containing the celebration pictures so many times that I sometimes believed I was actually there. I wasn't, of course, because I hadn't been born yet. Sometimes I wondered if I really had been there—in a previous life.

My uncles rented a long flat-bed truck and hauled my grandfather's totem pole all the way from western Canada to our back yard in Washington, D.C. They wanted my mother to have one of the family totem poles just like they did. We hired a crane operator to dig a hole and get the totem pole into the ground far enough to be supported. It seemed to take forever. My mother and I stayed safely inside and watched through the window as my uncles, my father and the crane operator struggled to get the massive totem pole into position. Even though I was probably no more than two or three years old at the time, I can still see and hear the grating of the giant chains and the truck lifting it high enough to get it into the ground. The totem pole seemed to reach clear up to the heavens.

The next day, all of us and a few of the curious neighbors held a welcoming ceremony for the totem pole. My uncles presided over the event. Uncle Takus began with his prayer, "Oh, Creator, we ask you to give this totem pole the power to protect its new family just as it has protected ours." Uncle Mulligan continued, "May all the animals of this totem provide wisdom and eternal life to all who visit." I still remember how tiny I felt compared to the totem pole. None of us could have known the figures depicted on the totem pole represented a portent of things to come. They really were destined to watch out for us.

That was one of the few times my uncles visited our home in Washington. After overseeing the totem pole placement and a day for sightseeing, they headed back to their lives in Canada. I still remember how I loved sitting on their laps while they told me stories. They were much larger men than my father and seemed like giants to me. As I came to realize, they were giants with their families, their tribe, their community and within themselves. They took such pride in their culture.

My uncle Takus asked, "Do you know how totem poles begin life?" "No, I don't," I answered. He continued, "Totem poles start out as extremely large trees, usually red cedar. After careful selection that can sometimes go on for weeks, the tree is cut down and the trunk is transported to wherever the artist is going to work on his artistic creation. The trunk is then stripped of its bark. Artists begin their storytelling with the pictures they chisel and carve into the tree trunk. It can take up to a year of work for the trunk to be transformed into a totem pole. An artist must never tell anyone else the story of the totem pole artistry, because it's considered bad luck. The animal or animals on a totem pole are supposed to join their human tribe in a mutual, protective bonding. The purpose of raising a totem pole is to show that humans and nature belong to a single order." Living up to all that responsibility was a pretty tall order for any totem pole, and maybe that's why they needed to be so huge.

I stared for hours at the totem pole in our back yard when I was a child. It had two human-like faces, one male and one female. It had a large bird, a large fish, and an even larger wolf. Sometimes the wolf's face took on human characteristics if I stared at it long enough. During one of our trips to Canada, I got to meet the artist who carved our totem pole. He was elderly by then and told me he learned his art from his father and grandfather. We talked about the totem pole. He was careful not to reveal its meaning. In my early teens I would have to go through a life-threatening rite of passage to understand the story behind the totem pole.

(See APPENDIX to Chapter Seven in back of book to learn more about the history of Canada's relationship with its natives and the life and art of the Kwakiutls.)

Chapter Eight
Grandfather Medici, Aborigines, and Blue Eyes

When I was nine, we got a call from one of my grandfather's business partners. "Calls during the middle of the night are never good news," my mother remarked the next morning. My Australian grandfather, Emilio, had suffered a heart attack and had been taken to a hospital. He had never remarried after the death of my grandmother, Gina, and my father was his next of kin. My father immediately booked us a flight to Melbourne, Australia. I felt an overwhelming sense of foreboding during the long airplane flight. When we got to the hospital, my grandfather asked my father in a voice raspier than usual, "Dom, can you go to the house and get the will from the safe and bring it to me?" My mother stayed in my grandfather's room at the hospital while my father and I drove to the house to retrieve the will. She said, "War-ne-la, ride along with your father and remind him to stay on the left side of the road." I would have to say, "Left side of the road, please," about every other turn. My father was often absent-minded, but it was obvious to me that he had something serious on his mind during the drive to my grandfather's house and back to the hospital. He barely acknowledged my presence in the car, which was uncharacteristic of his usual behavior. Normally, we were always chatting up a storm.

On the way back to the hospital I suddenly realized that I was starving and remembered that I hadn't eaten since we got off the plane. I had to physically turn my father's head toward me at a stop sign to ask, "Could we please stop at a pub and get some food for all of us so we don't have to eat the hospital food?" My father's gaze returned to me from whatever place he had been in his mind, and he agreed to stop at the neighborhood pub.

When we arrived back at the hospital, my grandfather had fallen asleep. My father sat in the chair and appeared to be lost in his thoughts. We ate our lunch mostly in silence. After finishing his fish and chips, my father opened the envelope retrieved from the safe in my grandfather's house and began to read its contents.

I watched his face, and observed how he alternated from a smile to a surprise and then a frown as he read the document in his hand. What was he reading that would create such a mixture of reactions? I'd never seen my father look the way he did that day in the hospital. His face became almost contorted as he absorbed the information in the will. This time, I couldn't get a sense of what was going on inside his head.

My mother and I had to wait until my grandfather awakened to find out what the will said.When he did, we found out the real story. Medici wasn't the family's real name after all. When my paternal grandfather's family left Italy after World War II, they made a decision to change their family name. My father told me later that the original Italian family had some unsavory connections in the Old World. I figured it must have been because they supported Italy's war-time leader, Benito Mussolini. I always meant to ask my father if he ever discovered any other living descendants of the original Italian family, but apparently it wasn't important enough for either of us to pursue. I thought that someday I would travel to Italy and visit the area where the Medicis figured so prominently. While there I would also tour the region where my grandparents grew up.

Okay, so we had an adopted name, according to the information in my grandfather's will. Lots of people changed their names when they moved to new countries. An adopted name didn't seem like such a big deal to me. But there was more information in the will. My grandparents had adopted my father from an orphanage for native Australian children. They had never told him he was adopted. My father also realized that his father had fibbed to him about his mother's heritage. Now my father was faced with the knowledge that he had more than just a little Aboriginal blood from his biological mother. His biological father had been part Aborigine also. Many Aboriginal children had been forcefully removed from their parents and their native lands, just as had happened with my mother's people in Canada. The different expressions on my father's face as he absorbed this new information about his heritage, which was also my heritage, was proving a bit difficult to comprehend.

As the time wore on in my grandfather's hospital room, I was feeling somewhat overwhelmed trying to figure out who I was and what the inheritance from the Aborigine side of the family meant for my future. I admit to some disappointment at the realization that I wasn't part Italian after all. How could I love Italian food so much if it wasn't "in my blood?"

In the hospital bookstore, I had purchased a book, *Message stick: contemporary Aboriginal writing* and located a poem that I thought captured the dilemma the Aborigines felt about what had happened to their native land.

Hawk and the Aborigine

I see you soaring above
Hunting just like me
You looking for food
Me searching for identity.

Only once you flew above
While I hunted down here
Gone are the tucker of survival
No longer I carry my hunting spear.

You keep soaring in the blue yonder
I'll search the legends of the caves
You look for something to eat
I'll search for lost tribal graves.

I see you swoop down on your prey
Me, I can't find any signs or trace
No marks or relics laying around
Of my once tribal Aboriginal race.

Civilizations, tractors, graders, ploughs
Have destroyed all signs of yesteryear
No animals, no yams, foliage vanished
Almost impossible to survive out here.

Hawk still you soar searching from above
Small lizards, insects will keep you alive
Me, I'll have to turn to white civilization
To make sure my tribal dreaming and stories survive.

By Cec Fisher

When my grandfather awakened from his nap, he motioned for my mother to come closer. He held both her hands and spoke to her very softly. I heard him say, "Dom's a good man. I never had to worry that you wouldn't take good care of him. Make sure you both look after War-ne-la. She has that 'miwi,' but she still needs both of you."

I remembered when I was smaller hearing my grandfather ask me, "Hey, Little Bambino, is your 'miwi' telling you when I'm going to die?" He often interjected Italian words and phrases into his speech, so I naturally assumed the word, "miwi" was Italian. I responded with another question, "What does the word 'miwi' mean? My grandfather replied, "It means that you're extra smart.

You'll understand better when you get older." It seemed like people were always telling me I would understand more things as I got older. I had previously asked my father, "What does Grandpapa mean when he says I have 'miwi'?" My father had answered, "It's that thing you have. He calls what you have 'miwi.' You know what he means, don't you?" The conversation ended there. My father and I were reluctant to discuss "that thing" I had. Imagine my surprise during my teenage years when I found out that "miwi" wasn't an Italian word at all, but a native Aboriginal word. 'Miwi' is the energy that gives a person psychic, or mental, power.

My grandfather was growing weaker at the hospital. The second day we were there he called me over to his bedside and took both of my hands in his, and I was so happy that he could still muster a twinkle in his eye. It was always so comforting to be around him, and being in a hospital room with him hadn't changed that comfort zone. He said, "Be careful how you use that 'miwi,' little blue eyes." I kissed his cheek, trying to hold back my tears. Then he said, "We'll see each other again soon. I'm not leaving you for very long." I responded, "Grandpapa, what do you mean?" He said, "You'll see. I'm going to take a nap now." I was left to think about our conversation the rest of the afternoon and wonder if others could tell I had any kind of special gift. Somehow I knew that my grandfather was probably right, that he wasn't leaving for good. I just didn't know how or when we would see each other again—not yet.

The sense I had that day in the hospital was that my grandfather was asking my father's forgiveness for not telling him earlier of his biological parentage, but I couldn't be sure because I couldn't hear much of their conversation. The only thing I was able to sense was a sort of darkness around both of them. My father, a gentle and kind man, with dark eyes that seemed to see everything, said, "It's all right, Papa. I understand. You can go in peace. Think about seeing Mother again." It looked to me like my father was in another world. I wondered some years later if my father also possessed some shamanic skills to ease my grandfather's leaving. As my grandfather's breathing became more labored, my father got up from the chair and sat on the bed. He held my grandfather in his arms as he left the bounds of earth. That was the only time

I ever saw my father cry. My mother must have used an entire box of tissues wiping her eyes and nose, but I could tell she was trying to stay composed for my father's sake.

During the time at the hospital, I stayed in the background. I felt like I was intruding on sacred ground somehow. I shed my own tears for the loss of my grandfather. I remembered his mustache and the twinkle in his eyes as we read to each other during our visits. I loved to hear his accent. It was part Old World and part Australian. He was a well-read man, and each time I visited, he would ask, "What are you learning in your American school and what books have you read lately?" I'll always remember the fabulous Italian dinners he served. He prepared dishes never found on menus in restaurants. Australia has an agricultural economy with fresh meat and vegetables readily available. I think sometimes he just threw his home-made pasta into the mix for tradition's sake. I wondered if I'd ever be able to cook as well as he did.

There were times during our visits to Australia when my parents would go off "on holiday" for a few days, and my grandfather and I would spend time at the family vineyards. He often engaged visitors at the tasting room and couldn't talk about the wines without practically dancing. It was always fun to hear the Australian, Italian and other accents whirling around. We also spent a lot of time in his kitchen. He never minded the messes I made as I helped him get a meal on the table. It took us as long to clean up the kitchen afterwards as it did to prepare the meal. I got to stand on a stool and wash while he rinsed and dried the dishes and pans. He usually drank the rest of the bottle of wine he had opened for dinner as we finished getting the kitchen back to normal. That's when he would tell me stories about his childhood in Italy and the activities of his family members during their early years in Australia. He didn't seem to mind my constant questions interrupting his stories. He was very patient in answering me, and he never seemed to lose his train of thought and where he was in his stories.

The story that made an impression on me was when he was about ten and got into a little mischief with some of the neighborhood boys. They had stolen some money from the horsecart driver who delivered their milk. Once the boys were caught, my grandfather didn't confess to his part in the caper, and when

my great-grandfather discovered his complicity in the crime, he threw him out of the house. He said, "I am so ashamed of the dishonor you have brought upon the family." Later that night my grandfather returned home and asked for a piece of bread. His father told him, "No, you may not have any bread or anything else because you have not learned your lesson about the importance of truthfulness and the family's honor." By the time my grandfather turned and walked away from the house for the second time, a basket of bread, cheeses and meats had mysteriously appeared on the path, just beyond my great-grandfather's view.

His father might have been trying to teach his boy a lesson, but no Italian mother would ever let her son go hungry. At that point in the story my grandfather let out one of his booming laughs and said, "Once I finally apologized, everyone made up and the family was okay again." I never minded doing the dishes at his house, because he made the time fly with his storytelling.

My grandfather never told the same story twice. I wasn't sure if he was making them up or if they really happened as he told them. I began to realize that it was truly a blessing to be the longest surviving member of your generation. You could tell the stories any way you wanted, and there was nobody left to refute your version. I wanted to live that long too. How could you ever forget a grandfather who let you think you were the most important person in the world to him? Everything he said and did was from a warm, kind heart. The last two days of his life were a gift for all of us, even if they were long. We got to say our good-byes to a man who maintained his sense of humor through adversity, had genuine curiosity of the world about him, and was humble yet had extraordinary strength of character. And above all, he cared deeply for his family. In the vast landscape of memories, he was a source of inspiration for all who knew him. I thought about it later, and realized I had traveled through more than seventy-five years with all my reminiscing. No wonder those two days had seemed so long.

Several times my grandfather had asked me, "Did you get your blue eyes from the stork that brought you?" Lots of people asked me where I got my blue eyes. I never knew how to answer the question.

(See APPENDIX to Chapter Eight at back of book to learn more about the Medici family, post-war Italy, and the early days of the Italians who migrated to Australia.)

Chapter Nine
Entertaining, Celtic Faeries, and a Pacific Ocean Tidal Wave

My childhood continued in what I thought was a normal, fun-filled and exciting manner. I traveled often with my parents, went with Kilmer to the swimming pool at the YWCA, ran through Rock Creek with her and the pets, and spent a lot of time reading—all after my assigned household chores were finished, of course. There was no question that I was somewhat an indulged child, accepting my good fortune without question. Most of the time I also accepted my unusual perceptive abilities as a normal part of my life, hearing and seeing things that others could not. And, as I got older, I began to realize that things seemed to happen for a reason. Maybe I needed to see both sides of the economic scale before I could appreciate my calling. Perhaps my comfortable home and loving parents facilitated the path toward understanding additional dimensions of life that few others experience. The groundwork was being set for my adult role—traveling all over the world helping disadvantaged people. But, as a child, I didn't quite realize that.

I loved helping my parents entertain. It seemed that we were always preparing for some function at our house. That's how I came to love cooking, especially the native dishes from my parents' countries and from other countries as well. Our cookbook collection filled an entire closet off the kitchen. I think they bought one in every country they visited. We weren't always able to locate the ingredients for the recipes, but we learned to improvise. I loved our trips to the rural farmers' markets for the fresh produce. Washington had lots of markets that catered to the world-wide shopping needs of its citizens. The Asian and African markets were probably my favorites. Uli taught all of us how to cook the African foods, and we learned together how to use a wok and cook Asian foods. We frequently ate Oriental style, sitting on big pillows around our big square coffee table. I mastered eating with chopsticks, after dropping food on my clothes, the table and the floor numerous times. I usually was allowed to stay up later when we had company and almost always enjoyed meeting and getting to know our guests. Following the example observed from my mother, I found someone who wasn't talking to anyone else and asked that person if I could get him or her something to eat or drink. This usually led to further conversation. My mother often said to people, "Whoever passed out the shy genes must have missed War-ne-la."

I was unaware, until someone else pointed it out, that I had begun talking like an adult as soon as I learned how to form words. Except for spending a lot of time around Kilmer, I was raised with adults who never spoke baby talk to me. So conversing like an adult was natural for me.

My mother said that **Dr. Eileen Burke**, one of her

university colleagues, always asked, "Will War-ne-la be there, m'Dear?" Only after my mother assured her, "Why, yes, of course she'll be here," would Dr. Burke accept the invitation to our home. I'm sure she was trying to flatter my mother. Everyone was always "m'Dear" to her. It must have been an Irish thing. Dr. Burke played the piano, too, so we often sat together on the piano bench and talked, sang and took turns playing while the rest of the guests wandered around our big comfortable house. She helped me figure out ways to stretch my small fingers to reach all the keys.

I remember the two of us laughing a lot together. She was always teaching me something new, like tying the laces from my tennis shoes together so I could carry them in my hand more easily. Just before dessert was served, she would say, "Come with me, m'Dear." Then she would lead me over to a box of chocolate candy she had brought, and she and I would take turns figuring out which ones had the softest insides, our favorite kind. If we guessed wrong, we'd put the chocolate back into the box and try another one. When we had worked our way through about half of the box, she would close the box and put it back in her purse before any other guests saw what we had been doing, and say, "M'Dear, we'll just put these away for later." It was one of several fun secrets we shared.

Dr. Burke's parents had come to America from Ireland, and I loved listening to her Irish brogue. She had focused on education and taught Renaissance Literature at the university. She had never married, as far as anyone knew. I sometimes thought of her as a grandmother. Since I didn't get to know either of my own grandmothers, she filled the role nicely.

When Dr. Burke retired, my mother hosted a Sunday afternoon tea for their colleagues from American University. Dr. Burke and I practiced a song which we performed for the guests during the tea party. Her opening to the group was, "Now, m'Dears, War-ne-la and I are going to perform a wee bit of a song for you today." I played the piano while she sang. It was an Irish ballad she had learned from her family about leaving your true love and hoping you never have to experience those sad feelings again. I noticed a few eyes being dabbed during the song. I couldn't tell if she was suggesting that her true love was teaching or a person from her past.

I wondered if Irish songs made people cry because they were remembering the heartbreaking stories of their ancestors. Many of them either starved in Ireland during the potato famine or were subjected to discrimination if they were fortunate enough to make it to America.

Dr. Burke once told me that the Irish surely saved civilization because they took in many of the educated people from the mainland of Europe when they were expelled from their own countries during the Dark Ages. She repeated the stories from her ancestors about seeing people hiding behind the trees, usually looking for something to eat. Those stories made their way into Irish folklore.

One year Dr. Burke gave me a book about Ireland for my birthday. She said, "After you've finished reading the book, I want to discuss it with you." My favorite chapter was about Celtic shamanism. Many of the ancient people of Ireland were known as Celts, with the hard *C* pronunciation, like in the word *candy*. Some of those people hiding behind the trees came to be known as nature spirits and were called *fairies*. The English word *fairy* comes from the Old French *faerie*, which came from the Latin *fata*, meaning *fate*. I wondered if my fate was somehow connected to those *faeries* of old Ireland. It is possible that I am part Irish on my father's side. During the Irish Potato Famine in the late 1840's many Irish deliberately committed a crime so they could be imprisoned and then shipped off to Australia. Perhaps one of them cavorted with an Aborigine in my ancestry. I sort of like it that I'll never solve the mystery of who gave me my blue eyes.

The only fairy I remembered from my childhood was the tooth fairy. He always knew when I lost a tooth and would leave some money in a little box just outside my bedroom door. The tooth fairy was just another spirit to me.

According to the Celtic shamanism chapter in the book that Dr. Burke gave me, the spirits running through the woods were fairy shamans, also known as storytellers, jokers, shapeshifters, seers, mediators between the mystical and the living, mythological goddesses or gods and healers. In the ancient and still-spoken Gaelic tongue of Ireland, their shamanic journeys were called *immrama*. Anyone going on a Celtic shamanic journey goes into a meditative state and surrounds himself with white light. Then he visualizes himself standing beside a well or a pond, throwing any problems into the water and watching it close over

him. It's a symbolic release that tells his subconscious that he needs an answer to solve a problem. Then he visualizes hiimself walking away from the water, leaving the problems behind. He can choose a nature scene for the inner journey about to be undertaken. After a few deep breaths and complete relaxation, the journey can begin.

Dr. Burke's favorite poet was William Butler Yeats, who died just before World War II began. She said, "Yeats said if you scratch any person deep enough you find a visionary, but that the Celt is a visionary without scratching." From the earliest recorded portions of their history, the Celtic peoples were considered excellent prophets and foretellers. Dr. Burke said, "The first time I saw the faeries as a little girl was after I had disobeyed my mother. They had arrived to help me figure out how to ask her for forgiveness. After that, they appeared whenever I was having a problem."

Dr. Burke continued to come over several times a year after her retirement, and we continued to play the piano together. Her first question as soon as she took off her wrap would be, "How many faeries have we seen lately, and what have they taught you, m'Dear?" The response invariably led to a discussion of her latest trip to someplace in the world. I fancied that I might travel to Ireland with her one day so I could have something of a formal introduction to the faeries of the "Emerald Isle." My list of places to visit grew longer every time we had guests. I wanted to see the whole world!

My vivid dreams didn't always go smoothly during my childhood. It was not unusual for me to wake up during the night covered with perspiration after I'd been trekking over Thailand on the back of an elephant or riding a camel across the Arabian Desert. I would be so sure I had been where my dreams had taken me that I would have to turn on the lamp next to my bed to be sure I was in my own room. My hand seemed to travel to the light switch all by itself. I didn't want anyone to know that I dreamed of happenings before they took place. I wondered if it was possible that I was somehow willing events to happen so my dreams would come true.

I once dreamed of a tidal wave that traveled over the Pacific Ocean to the shores of Canada and inundated the villages where my mother's Kwakiutl family lived. The next morning I asked my mother, "Have we talked to our Canadian family recently?" She said, "No, not in several weeks." And then I asked, "Do you think we could call them to make sure they're all right?" Mother asked, "Is there something specific you're worried about?" "Yes," I said. "I dreamed a big wave came in at high tide and flooded their land." She agreed to place the call. We were unable to get through for several days. When we finally did, our relatives relayed the story of a tidal wave that had just hit their area during the week and leveled some of the buildings closer to the shore. My mother ascertained that everyone had been accounted for and that their electric power had been restored. As she hung up the phone, she asked me to be sure to let her know if I ever again had disaster dreams involving anyone we knew. I promised her I would. I was feeling better each time my intuition or a dream about something turned out to be based on something factual because I felt that meant the spirits were definitely communicating with me.

The good dreams were of people coming to visit or something happening in the family or neighborhood that came true. The nightmares were of fires in Australia and drought in Canada, all of which also came true. My feelings vacillated between reconciling myself to having dreams that foretold the future to trying hard to forget the ones that caused suffering so they wouldn't come true. Once the dreams were recorded in my dream journal, it was easier to let go of their memories and not think about them as much. I sort of hoped that by recording the dreams in my journal I could leave them there. Sometimes it worked, but other times they leaped from the pages of the journal into reality.

A frequent dream I had was being on a ship that ran aground in bad weather and broke apart. The shipwreck, passengers and animals and I were all washed ashore by the action of the tides and waves. I felt the waves washing over me as I was pushed and pulled toward the shoreline. Various animals would help get me out of the waves and up onto the shore. I would feel them nudging me toward the shore and sometimes dragging me with their teeth clamped onto my soggy clothes. In one dream, a fellow passenger grabbed hold of my long hair, the only part of me he could reach, and pulled me toward the shore. The subconscious fear of drowning was so strong and pervasive that I woke up gasping for air. I couldn't figure out why this same dream with a few variations visited me so often.

In other dreams I fell out of airplanes, waking up before I hit the ground. My heart would be racing and my whole body perspiring and shaking from the ordeals of my subconscious mind. My nighttime terrors happened frequently. When I turned the light on, they went away. It took awhile for me to breathe normally again and fall back to sleep.

Whenever I told my parents of my wild dreams, they would suggest I read more peaceful stories before falling asleep. If only it were that simple.

I kept trying to understand the meaning of my dreams. Were my dreams telling me that the ability to communicate telepathically (between minds) with animals and people was being given to me so I could see and hear what others couldn't? And if I did have that ability, what was its purpose? How would that knowledge and ability be put to use? Would it be used for good, or could it also be evil? Would people think I was crazy and have me institutionalized? Why was I chosen to receive this special gift? I discovered that people often fear what they are unable to understand. If you can't see or touch something, does it really exist? Could others tell that I could sense what they were thinking and could "see" people and animals around them that they couldn't? Would people be uncomfortable if they knew of my special abilities? My childhood seemed to be filled with questions that went on forever.

Chapter Ten
Animal Spirit Helpers and the Hand of Fate

Traveling with my parents provided a great deal of my education, the kind you don't get in school. Whenever we packed for a trip, I helped pack my bags. After the clothes were packed, we put in my flashlight, extra batteries, schoolbooks and supplies. Then we took turns putting in extras. I put in something I'd chosen, usually a book, and my mother or father put in something wrapped up in plain brown paper. We counted one for each day we were going to be away. If it was a long flight, I got one for the flight too. They wanted something to occupy me while I sat in the back of the classroom during their lectures. They may have thought I didn't like listening to their lectures and the class participation, but to me, their classrooms provided another opportunity to learn what people were thinking and doing in whatever country we were visiting. I didn't understand everything in the adult classrooms, but I always learned and remembered something.

As I got older, I began to visit university libraries. I usually went to the sections on art, medicine and history. When I found a book on native medicine, I wrote down the title and author. When I got back home, I would ask our school or public library to borrow it if they didn't have it on the shelves. Sometimes the librarians had to go to other states to locate the book. If they couldn't locate it, my parents sometimes bought it for me if they thought it was worthwhile. I took notes of what I learned from the borrowed library books and kept them in a notebook in my bookcase, along with the gifts of native healing books and my handwritten journals.

My favorite topic for dinnertime discussion was healing with what is naturally in the environment. That's how I originally learned about herbs. I loved the smell of the different scents coming from our herb garden. The herbs were planted near our totem pole. While preparing dinner, my parents would often hand me a pair of kitchen scissors and tell me which ones to snip and bring in to season the food they were cooking. That's how I learned to distinguish the different plants. I loved tasting them on the way back to the house. The herbs that we grew for healing purposes were harvested, dried and placed in special glass containers. We had our own herbal medicine chest in a pantry off the kitchen. I soon realized that learning about the healing power of herbs would require a lifetime of continuing education.

The first time I nearly lost my life was during a trip with my parents to Central America when I was almost eleven. I became ill with a rapidly elevating temperature and had to be hospitalized. The doctors were unable to figure out the cause of my illness. As a precaution, they started me on an antibiotic regimen. Apparently I was hallucinating and describing strange visions in my semi-conscious state. I saw a white wolf circling in the darkness, around a large black hand on a white background. White on black and black on white pierced my dreams. The wolf howled frequently, and whenever she got close enough, licked one of the black fingers of the hand of fate. Part of me could feel her licking my hand.

There was also a camel racing across a sandy desert with me on its back clad in a white sheet. I could feel him under me and the bumpy and uneven gait as he ran. I had to hold on with all my strength to keep from falling off. Once when I woke up the bed was still shaking. There was also a huge hawk that kept a vigil at the window near my bed. If I dozed off for too long, he would emit a shrill cry to awaken me. As soon as I woke up and saw him, he would fly away and disappear from view. I don't remember much about my stay in the hospital, except an occasional awareness that my parents were bathing my over-heated body with ice cold wet washcloths in an effort to lower my body temperature. The doctors and my parents were concerned that the high fever might affect my brain. My mother often reverted to the native ways of doctoring. She knew the fever was helping fight an infection in my body, but she wanted to diminish any harmful effects from it. She insisted that the best way to lower the temperature of the blood was to keep the skin cold so that the blood flowing under the cooled skin would then cool. I have a vague memory of them singing softly while I was lying in the hospital bed. Perhaps they were just trying to pass the time and keep

their minds occupied with something besides my illness. Maybe they were trying to give my brain something to focus on besides the strange visions.

My parents didn't talk to me about what happened during my stay in the hospital until I became a teenager. I didn't realize until they talked to me about the visions I had described to them that my animal spirit helpers had chosen that time to introduce themselves. In the intervening years I visited those same spirits many times during my meditative shamanic journeys. The white wolf became my power animal and protector. The camel transported me anywhere I traveled. The hawk enhanced the vision of my blue eyes. The spirits visited me often. I've wondered if that fever had anything to do with my extrasensory perception. Some anthropologists and neurologists have speculated that Black Elk, the Oglala Sioux shaman, may have received his healing powers during the time in his childhood when he was ill with a high fever.

Later on I began to wonder if perhaps there were no medical diagnoses for feverish illnesses. Perhaps it was nature's way of imparting abilities to us that we couldn't get any other way. The early settlers of North and South

America were overly focused on taking whatever land they could, resulting in the destruction of the native culture before learning about their centuries-old connection to nature and the earth. I wondered if we were now being given other means of rediscovering what they knew instinctively and if it was Mother Nature's way of reminding us that it is the great spirits who are in charge of the earth.

At the hospital in Central America, my parents took turns staying with me. My mother taught her classes and then drove straight to the hospital to relieve my father. They only slept long enough to refresh themselves, after which they returned to the hospital. After six days of fever and hovering near death, I got better. The antibiotics must have killed whatever infection had invaded my body, helping the fever to subside. I stayed in the hospital for a total of eight days before the doctors released me. As my mother helped me get dressed, she said, "War-ne-la, we're leaving for home, and as far as I'm concerned, we can't get there fast enough."

The pathology report from the hospital arrived in our mail several weeks later. Microscopic tropical bacteria had decided to enter my system and set up housekeeping for themselves and their descendants. The bacteria wanted to stay in my body, but we wanted them to leave. New medicine forced their early demise; old medicine kept damaging side effects to a minimum. Although the whole experience was scary for me, and no doubt for my parents as well, I felt that some hand of fate had intervened to keep me alive. My awareness that other forces and powers were influencing my development was quite vivid. There just had to be a reason those animal spirits made themselves known to me while I was in the hospital. They would soon become a part of who I was.

A visible representation of the hand of fate that might have played a part in saving my life presented itself in a startling fashion once we arrived home. During the time we were in Central America, a terrible storm had hit our area. Many of our trees had been damaged, and whole limbs were lying everywhere in the yard. One large limb had fallen near the meditation circle in the back of our yard. The limb looked like a giant dark hand and forearm. We all stopped in our tracks at what we considered an omen or sign from somewhere. For once we were all speechless.

My talented parents decided to incorporate the limb, which we came to call the "hand of fate," into an art display right where it had fallen from the tree. My father prepared the slight grade of the ground by first clearing it of its vegetation and then covering the area with a dark plastic tarp. He ordered a load of white stone which was rather unceremoniously dumped in our driveway. My father then covered the tarp with the stones. Kilmer and I got to help him shovel the stones into the wheelbarrow. Then we ran alongside him as he transported the stones from the driveway to the back yard. On the way back to the driveway for another load of stone, we took turns getting a ride in the wheelbarrow.

My father painted the hand with a clear acrylic paint to preserve the wood. He said, "If the wood isn't sealed and preserved, it will decay within a few years. Decayed wood returns to the earth to give birth to something new, and we want our hand of fate to be around for awhile, don't we?" A few days later my father gave the wood a second coat and let it dry. Once the stones were all in place, he laid the hand of fate on top of the stones, carefully anchoring it so it would stay in place. The contrast of the dark wood on the white stones was dramatic, just like in my dreams.

Uli, Kilmer, my parents and I held a little dedication ceremony for the new addition to our meditation circle. The dark hand on the white stones became quite a conversation piece over the years. It's still in the yard, a tangible reminder of unknown outside forces that look after us. It continues to provide significant comfort for our family. Even as an adult, the first thing I do after arriving at my parents' home is to visit the meditation circle with the totem pole, the hand of fate and the herbs. Once I'm centered, I touch the hand to receive its cosmic energy and blessings. I stand in the circle with my eyes closed, sometimes for quite a while, as I receive its energy. Then I am rejuvenated enough to continue with my life's journey.

Chapter Eleven
First Shamanic Healing Experience with New Teacher

Shamans (pronounced *SHAH-maans*) are the medicine men and women in many tribal cultures. They are doctors of the soul who are concerned about the spiritual health of individuals. Their specialty is inducing an altered or different state of awareness or consciousness, using all sorts of rituals. Rituals to achieve an altered state can involve drumming and music, communion with nature and sometimes even the ingestion of psychedelic power plants, such as mushrooms. Deprivation of water and food for an extended period can also induce an altered state of awareness.

The purpose of going into an altered state of consciousness is to receive a vision that will help heal an individual by putting him or her in touch with the spirits, their ancestors. The sick individual may be at odds with nature. The spirit world and this world have somehow become unbalanced. The shaman is called upon to restore harmony between the individual and his or her environment. It is not unusual for the shaman and the sick individual to go into a trance during the healing ceremony.

The word "shaman" comes from the Tungus reindeer herders of Siberia, which is a part of Russia and covers the continents of Europe and Asia. It means "wise one" or "one who knows" or "one who sees in the dark." Derivations of the root word *saman* are found all over the world. A shaman is someone who has mastered spirits and can, at will, introduce these spirits into themselves. Shamans use their power over the spirits for their own interests and to help people or communities that are suffering or need some type of assistance in their lives. The practice of shamanism is the oldest method people have used to find a connection to their creation. The practice has been traced back to the Stone Age, about 50,000 years ago. Shamanism is in our roots, no matter where we live. Probably all of us have evolved from some type of shamanic culture. It represents our cosmology, the search for our place in the universe. Shamans have supernatural powers that are not restricted to healing. Some cultures refer to them as seers, spiritual mediums or rain-makers.

If shamanism was considered the basis on which most of the world's religions were founded, what does that say about the founders of those religions? As I got older, I studied the different religions and paid particular attention to any spirit references.

(See APPENDIX ONE to Chapter Eleven at back of book to learn more about the world's religions and their similarities to shamanism.)

With shamanism so prevalent in the cultures of both sides of my ancestry, I didn't have much chance of escaping its embrace. How could I have imagined that all these conscious and unconscious forces in the universe would converge within my still-growing body? Could that have been what my vivid dreams were trying to tell me? Was there an explanation for why there were times when I couldn't tell which world I was in? Sometimes I found myself struggling to figure out what dimension or world I was in at any given moment. Dreaming was one reality, but I always awakened from that world. I often had difficulty figuring out if I was in the same reality others around me could see, or in another reality which existed only in my mind? My mind roamed among all the levels of consciousness.

Were my vivid dreams a part of my father's Aboriginal Dreamtime heritage? The two of us often read and discussed various stories about the

Aboriginal Dreamtime. My favorites had to do with shamans and the ancestor spirits. My father said his favorite was the Southern Cross, a constellation with four brilliant stars that look like the four points of a Latin cross. It's almost always visible in the skies over Australia and is replicated in the national flag. The Dreamtime story says the Southern Cross constellation is a sign to men that there is a place for them in the limitless regions of space, the home of the All-Father himself, and that beyond death lies a new creation. My father once said, "I might have been an astronaut if I had been from a country with a space program." Then he laughed and said, "That's okay; it can wait until my next life."

My father and I were descended from the Aborigines, and I wondered if our minds and bodies had inherited some native wisdom and ability to survive. Were my dreams trying to help me identify more strongly with my Aboriginal heritage?

The spirits often spoke to me, and I frequently felt their presence. Except for occasions when my mind was focused on something else and I didn't want to communicate with them, I was getting more and more comfortable with the spirits every day. My quest to understand the spiritual side of my life continues to the present day. I have learned that when the student is ready to learn, the teacher appears.

My parents permitted me to attend a local introductory shamanism workshop one weekend when I was about twelve. It was sponsored by the Foundation for Shamanic Studies, which was founded by a man named Michael Harner. One of our assignments was to locate and identify our teacher during one of our meditative drumming journeys. The workshop leader did the drumming while the rest of us closed our eyes and went on the shamanic journeys for the particular purpose stated by the instructor.

I waited to find out who appeared as my teacher, and when I asked,

"Are you my teacher?" he answered, "Yes, I am." Imagine my surprise when my teacher turned out to be my deceased Australian grandfather, Emilio Medici. Now I had someone I remembered well who would be able to help me learn what I needed to know to continue with my life. The spiritual world wasn't quite so intimidating now because I had someone guiding me who had always provided me with a great deal of comfort. Even though he was gone from my life physically, he could still be with me in the spiritual world. I remembered that as he lay dying in the hospital in Australia he had told me he would see me before long. I knew I would have to wait to learn what he would teach me. I didn't have to wait very long.

Rock Creek Park consists of over 1700 acres, and I tried to explore all of it at one time or another, managing to get temporarily lost several times. I followed it pretty far north several times and thought that someday I would follow it as far north as it goes, somewhere in Pennsylvania. My first meeting with my teacher-grandfather during a shamanic experience happened during one of my many walks north through Rock Creek Park. I came upon a beautiful black and white feather lying at the bottom of a hill. My first thought was to pick it up and add it to our collection. In the library of our house, there were three crystal glass vases filled with feathers collected from all over the world. Most were tagged with identification, but we weren't sure what birds produced some of them. As I bent over to reach for the feather, something stopped my hand. The feather blew a little farther up the hill and seemed to be beckoning me to follow it. I immediately wondered if the holy wind, known as *nilchi* to the Navajos, was blowing the feather up the hill. I felt compelled to follow and shortly saw another feather. More feathers continued up to the top of the hill. None of the feathers wanted to be picked up, however. I knew instinctively that I was being led to someone or something.

As I got to the top of the hill, I came upon an apparition of a weeping young Algonquin Indian girl. I watched her for a little bit. She slowly looked toward me and then disappeared around the side of the hill. I followed and caught sight of her again. Standing about five or six feet behind her was my Australian teacher-grandfather. He motioned for me to walk toward the girl. I went to her and spoke to her in some language that was not my own. I didn't know where the language was coming from. The girl told me her young brave had been sent north to fight their enemies and had not returned, and she feared he had died in battle. She asked if I could help her locate him.

I can't remember being scared at that moment, but I must have been, because I remember trembling after I returned home. I asked the young girl if we could meditate together and perhaps journey to the battle site. I didn't have my drum or rattle with me, so we just closed our eyes for the journey to the battlefield. I could see a young brave being shot with an arrow and falling from his horse.

After a while we both opened our eyes. The young girl told me of the vision she had experienced during her journey. Our journeys had taken both of us to the same location. During her journey she ran to him after his fall from the horse and moved him out of the way of the battle. He died in her arms within a few hours. I realized as she was telling me the story of her journey that she had stopped weeping. She said that now she knew what she must do. She would travel to his family and bring them the terrible news of their son's death. Then she would take them to the site where she had buried him. After these two events took place, he would be free to pass through the light to the other world. Only then would she be free to join him. I didn't realize then that I was participating in a soul retrieval exercise. His soul needed to be recovered and reunited with hers before either of them could rest in eternal peace. She appeared to smile slightly and then disappeared from my view. I was filled with the realization that she had really healed herself from some type of energy that came from the earth. My teacher-grandfather and I just happened to be there to help her locate the needed energy. I never saw the feathers or the young Indian girl again. In fact, I couldn't locate exactly where in Rock Creek Park I had been when I saw the Indian girl. I realized that my first shamanic experience had taken place and then spent a long time wondering if my future would consist of experiences similar to communicating with the Algonquin Indian girl's apparition.

I walked back down the hillside and toward home. Upon my arrival into the kitchen, my mother exclaimed, "War-ne-la, you look like you've seen a ghost!"

I was often on a spiritual journey traveling a million miles from earth, engaged in some spiritual communication and eager to continue on that path. The drumming tape given to me by Uli would call me back with a change in the drumming cadence. Sometimes I was reluctant to return to earth. However, once I returned, there was usually something equally as exciting happening in my current real life. Then I would find myself reluctant to leave my current life to return to a spiritual journey. But I kept traveling between the two worlds, occasionally at dizzyingly fast intervals. The call of the spirit world was often seductive.

The universe apparently had plans for me. I wouldn't be able to be like everyone else or fit in with my peers. My destiny was to hold something quite different. The spirits continued calling me, and my intuition told me they were going to teach me about shamanism. Fighting to stay away from the spirit world and yet having an overwhelming desire to go there kept me awake many nights.

My parents often discussed their native legends, and I was always struck by the similarities between North American natives and Australian natives. If their ancestors were from different branches of mankind, how could their stories have so many of the same themes? When I asked my parents, "How can we in the United States preserve our stories for future generations?" They responded, "It can start with you."

As fate would have it, that process was about to begin with an experience on the Chesapeake Bay that brought my childhood to a crashing end and changed my life forever. But first, I had to survive another near-death experience.

(See APPENDIX TWO to Chapter Eleven at back of book to learn more about Aboriginal Culture and History.)

Chapter Twelve
Sailing Above (and Below) the Chesapeake Bay

My parents had long-time friends, **Frank and Jane Metitzo**, who kept their sailboat near their home on the Severn River in Annapolis, Maryland. Frank was a marine biologist and Jane taught future teachers at a local Maryland university. Jane and my mother met when my mother taught one of her counseling classes at the same university where Jane taught. Frank and Jane loved to sail every spare minute they could, as long as the weather cooperated. We were often invited to sail with them. I learned something new about sailing every time we went out. Sometimes Frank would let me take the wheel. He taught me to keep one eye on the depth gauge and one on a far distant landmark. What I learned just as I was turning thirteen had very little to do with sailing, however.

On a beautiful early summer Saturday, we boarded the sailboat for what looked to be the most glorious day of sailing yet. The wind was blowing briskly as we headed out to the Chesapeake Bay. On board were Frank and Jane, my parents and me, and Uli and Kilmer. Seven makes for a good crew, if we all do our parts. I admit to showing off a little bit to Kilmer as I helped her understand some of the details of the boat. This was the first time she and Uli had come with us on the sailboat. We all had swimsuits on under our clothes, and Frank made sure we were all wearing life jackets.

Annapolis sits right at the edge of the Chesapeake Bay, the northern hemisphere's largest estuary. Prior to the planet warming after the last Ice Age, it was the lower part of the Susquehanna River. The melting glaciers filled the valley with river water and salt water from the Atlantic Ocean. Now it is two hundred miles long and anywhere from three to thirty miles wide. It covers sixty-four thousand square miles, and it separates the Delmarva Peninsula from the mainland of Maryland and Virginia. It took me a little while to figure out that Delmarva was something of an acronym for the states of Delaware, Maryland and Virginia. All of Delaware and parts of Maryland and Virginia compose the land on that peninsula. The Chesapeake Bay is fed by many rivers, including the Susquehanna, Sassafras, Chester, Choptank, Nantikoke, Wicomico, Severn, Potomac, Rappahannock, York and James. If I went sailing every day until I'm a hundred years old, I would never see every inlet of the Chesapeake Bay. Four hundred years ago, Captain John Smith, the famous English navigator, explored and charted the Chesapeake Bay, the first European to do so. I wonder if I'll ever see as much of it as he did. I have always been curiously drawn to the area. I particularly liked the bird population, my favorite being the great blue heron. When they fly, their necks fold back on their shoulders. They're so elegant, no matter what they're doing. Perhaps I could choose a heron for my totem. The bird on the totem pole in our backyard looked a lot like the great blues of the Chesapeake Bay.

On a motorboat also in the water that day were members of a church group and their chaperones. We waved to each other across the water. None of us could have imagined that our paths were about to cross – really cross. We met quite unexpectedly in a rather dramatic fashion under unusual circumstances created by a sudden weather squall.

The Baptist Church of Greater Southeast Washington had raised money for a day's boat trip for their youth. On board the twenty-six-foot motorboat were two chaperones and twelve high school-aged youths. Many of the young people were from poor families, so raising the funds to finance the trip had taken place over several months.

The **Reverend Joseph Hutton** and his wife, **Abbe**, were the official and unofficial leaders of the church. He was the minister, and she was the choir director and organist. Both acted as mentors for the young people of their flock. Rev. Hutton was sitting in the first seat of the boat, and Abbe was sitting in the last seat. They had a pact to keep whoever they were chaperoning between them. Nobody could ever get lost from the group if each of them guarded their respective ends. He chivalrously led the way in case of danger, and she made sure everyone followed along as she brought up the rear. Roll call took place any time the group loaded or reloaded onto buses or cars or, in this case, boats. Rev. Hutton would call out, "Number One," and then each student called out the number he or she had pinned to their clothes. Then Abbe would call out her number, whatever the last one was. On this trip, she was "Number 14."

Our sailboat and their motorboat headed past the mouth of the Severn River and entered the Chesapeake Bay. We were barely out into the Bay when out of nowhere the wind that had been merely blowing briskly turned absolutely fierce, creating choppy waves all around us. Frank and Jane began immediately lowering the sails to stabilize the sailboat. Suddenly we heard a loud smacking noise as the motorboat carrying the church group hit something in the water. All of us on the sailboat watched in horror as the motorboat tipped completely over, spilling everyone out into the water. All of them were wearing life jackets, and we could hear their panicked cries for help over the noises of the storm. Even if they could swim, the waves were becoming dangerously high, making swimming almost impossible. There wasn't anyplace to swim toward anyway, except our sailboat. Not much would have been visible from their water level other than the waves rolling over them. Even though it was summertime, I knew the water was cold.

Frank immediately started the sailboat's motor and headed toward the overturned boat. It took only a few seconds to arrive at the scene because we were so close. While he steered the sailboat, Jane called in an SOS on the designated emergency radio channel for an emergency water rescue.

Without a word, but an exchange of our "knowing" look, my father and I tore off our shoes. He said, "Let's go," and we dove into the water. I barely had a chance to see my mother's worried look before diving off the sailboat. Kilmer saw what we were doing and jumped in the water right behind us. I vaguely heard Uli yelling something to Kilmer. If anyone else said anything, I didn't hear them.

The three of us formed a circle around the group and began encouraging them to stay calm. We told them we would help them onto the sailboat one at a time. It was difficult seeing all of them because the storm had darkened the skies quickly and the waves were high. Rev. Hutton was trying to count the young people to determine how many had been rescued. In the confusion, it was impossible to accomplish any orderly roll call. There had been no practice drills for a rescue operation like this. We would have to make it up as we went along. My father, Kilmer and I helped the passengers onto the transom of the sailboat. Frank was steadying and guiding the sailboat as close to us in the water as he could safely do so. Jane, Uli and my mother were helping them move from the transom farther onto the boat. By this time two other boats were on the scene helping with the rescue. That was good because the sailboat would have had difficulty accommodating all the rescued passengers.

Suddenly my teacher-grandfather appeared and guided me toward one of the passengers slumped over in her life jacket. His presence guided my hands and body as I carefully led her toward the sailboat. I would find out later that she was Abbe, the wife of Rev. Hutton. With my teacher-grandfather encouraging and guiding me, I tugged at her as gently as I could and paddled toward the sailboat with one arm pulling the top of her life jacket at the back of her neck and the other stroking the water toward the sailboat. It didn't seem like I was getting any closer to the sailboat as each wave rolled over us. It was a struggle to breathe and not wear myself out as I kept paddling toward the sailboat. She still wasn't paddling or moving on her own. I wondered if perhaps she wasn't still alive or if she had hit her head on the boat and been knocked unconscious. I kept silently saying, "Don't give up yet; you're almost there." As my father, Kilmer and I carefully lifted and shoved her onto the transom of the boat, I was suddenly swept away from all of them by a huge wave. My strong swimming skills and life jacket meant nothing against the churning water. The storm had darkened the skies to the point that I could barely see the sailboat. The last thing I remembered was everyone yelling at me as the rapidly moving water pulled me away from the sailboat and under the waves. My father stayed in the water trying to find me, but I couldn't see him. He couldn't see me either.

I don't have a clear memory of what happened next. I must have gone into an altered state of consciousness. Something had to change for me to be under the water more than a few minutes. The normal time humans can hold their breath is three to four minutes. The didgeridoo playing with its need for breath control took my father and me above the average. Part of me was thinking the buoyancy of my body and the life jacket would lift me up to the surface, but I don't believe it did.

My only awareness was of the currents carrying my body. Just like in the dreams, the waves kept crashing over me. But several things were different from the dreams. There was a huge fish like the one on our totem pole that kept ramming its nose under my body and pushing me toward the surface with its precious air. On top of the water was a great blue heron, also like the one on our totem pole. She kept pulling at the top of my life jacket with her beak whenever I floated near the surface. After awhile a dog that looked like the wolf on our totem pole was in the water with me. The "wolf" kept snarling and swimming under me, pushing me up on top of the waves for air and shoving me toward the shore. The wolf dog communicated to me that I should keep moving toward the shore.

Was that the legend on our totem pole? Was the totem pole foretelling the story of my life? Were the two people at the top, the bird, the fish and the wolf, leading me on a journey to an unknown destination? Had my dreams told me how my life would end? In my dreams, I had always awakened before I drowned. But this couldn't be a dream—could it? Whatever it was, I was not waking up and it was going on for a very long time.

Back at the sailboat, my parents, Jane and Frank, Uli and Kilmer were becoming increasingly frantic because they couldn't see me anywhere in the water. After a while, I had a vague awareness of hearing sirens in the distance as I was being pushed around in the water by my animal friends.

I was in the water for several hours before becoming vaguely aware of mud and sand beneath me. I struggled to crawl out of the water and onto the dry land. The barking wolf dog kept nipping and shoving and dragging me toward the shore. I was partially aware that my lungs were full of water. As I crawled out of the water and onto the land, I managed to get my head turned toward the water, so that the bottom half of my body was slightly higher than my head. I'm not sure I'd ever realized that lungs will drain if gravity can help the water run down hill and drain out through the mouth. At some level of consciousness, I apparently knew to get my body positioned for the gravity to work. I hadn't awakened from my dream yet. When would the dream end so I could wake up and turn the light on in my room? It was taking an awfully long time.

At some point in my dream or whatever level of consciousness I was in, I became aware of the sound of helicopters in the distance. The whirring blades became awfully loud and then the volume would lessen. Helicopters carrying the president and his family often flew over our house on their way from the White House to Camp David, located in Maryland's Catoctin Mountains. We had become so used to them that we rarely looked up anymore when they flew over. So if I could hear the helicopters, it could only mean that I had to be at home and would wake up from my dream any minute. Since I wasn't in danger of drowning any longer, why couldn't I wake up? I kept telling myself to wake up, but I couldn't. I could hear the wolf dog barking in my ear.

Frank managed to steer the sailboat under motorized power toward the dock to deposit his unexpected passengers for transfer to ambulances. The Coast Guard and other boats did the same with their rescued passengers. It was not safe to return to the crash site with the sailboat, much to my parents' distress. My father was sure he could somehow locate me in the water. The Naval Academy and the Anne Arundel County sheriff's office had loaned their helicopters for the rescue effort. My parents and Kilmer had been granted permission to ride along in the back seat of one of the helicopters, and they began looking for me from the air. When they couldn't find me near the crash site, the pilots widened their search circles. One helicopter circled back and forth across the Bay, heading downstream a little farther with each circle. The dark skies had brightened after the storm ended, aiding the pilots in their search. As dusk was settling in, the searchlights on one of the helicopters caught some movement on a beach area of Kent Island on the eastern side of the Chesapeake Bay. They could see what appeared to be a large black dog and something else near it.

The pilot and co-pilot carrying my parents and Kilmer landed their helicopter as close to the Chesapeake Bay as possible. I could hear my parents and Kilmer calling "War-ne-la, War-ne-la." Now I knew I would wake up since they would have to be with me in my room. The helicopter noise was still so loud, like it was right outside my window. The wolf dog was barking louder than ever.

Kilmer's strong track-running legs took the lead, with my parents close behind. The pilot and co-pilot, with their emergency bags thrown hastily over their shoulders, brought up the rear. My parents and Kilmer said later they thought the sight of my head lifting up from the sand must have been wishful thinking, because they had reluctantly reconciled themselves to the fact that they would be recovering my drowned body. My dream was over, and I was finally waking up. I turned over to reach for the lamp switch and got a cold, wet nose in my hand instead.

The aftermath of what happened is still a little blurry for me. My parents and Kilmer were grabbing at me and talking all at once. I couldn't seem to fathom why they were acting that way. The pilot radioed someone that I'd been located alive and needed the medical evacuation helicopter for transport to a hospital. I tried to get up and immediately fell back down onto the sand. The co-pilot was listening to my heart and lungs and ordered me to be still. Once they got me extracted from the soggy lifejacket, they wrapped my bleeding knee with a large white bandage and then wrapped blankets around me. I slowly began to realize that I was absolutely freezing and that my teeth were chattering.

The "medivac" helicopter landed near the other one. The crew had been on alert at the Naval Academy since Jane had broadcast the SOS. It took them only a few minutes to get to us. The crew brought a stretcher over to the sand

and set it down next to me. They all seemed to be doing something to some part of my body. I kept coughing, and they said that was good, to keep coughing. Water was still coming out of my lungs and exiting through my mouth. The "medivac" crew needed to be sure my vital signs were stable enough for me to be moved. I knew vaguely what blood pressure was and heard the crew tell my parents that mine was low. The chill I had felt was beginning to lessen under the warm blankets. I heard my father say "Good doggie" several times. As I was carried face-down on the stretcher toward the helicopter, my mother walked behind the stretcher, holding onto one of my toes through the blankets. That was the only part of my body she could reach. I couldn't see the wolf-dog anymore once I was lifted into the "medivac" helicopter.

As the helicopter door closed, my father said, "Do what they tell you now, and we'll meet you at the hospital." My mother winked with her left eye, but I'm not sure in my confused state if I returned the wink, though I know I tried. The pilot of the first helicopter promised to radio Frank, Jane and Uli that I had been located. I wanted to go to sleep, but the rescue team wasn't having any of that. They started an intravenous (I.V.) drip, and I tried really hard not to jump when the needle stuck the vein in my left arm. My mind still wasn't able to understand what was causing all the excitement and noise. I continued coughing up water from my lungs. Once the crew put an oxygen tube into my nose, I began to take in my surroundings a little more clearly.

Chapter Thirteen
Physical and Spiritual Healing

After Frank, Jane and Uli got the message that I had been rescued alive and my parents and Kilmer had been returned via helicopter to the Naval Academy, they all headed to Johns Hopkins University Hospital in Baltimore, Maryland. They were the only ones, along with my adopted grandmother, Dr. Eileen Burke, allowed into my room. When she came into the hospital room the first time, Dr. Burke said, "War-ne-la, m'dear, you've given us quite a fright, but I'm glad to see you looking so well. I've brought a box of our favorite chocolates!"

I had to stay at the hospital nearly a week for observation. I couldn't tell what they were trying to observe. I kept dozing off, and whenever I woke up, someone was holding on to some part of me. It seemed like every five minutes the nurses were placing the stethoscope on my chest and back to check my lungs. I got several tetanus and other shots in my rear. It was sore for days. I was allowed to get up only to use the bathroom, and then only if someone was supporting me. I just couldn't go in a bedpan. It took some effort to get me, the rolling piece of equipment supporting my I.V. line, and whoever was holding on to me into the little bathroom. After several days, I asked the doctor, "Am I healing and getting back to normal?" She said, "I can't tell absolutely, but you seem to be recovering without any medication." I decided that must be good news.

I was taken out of the room for several examinations of my head, a positron emission tomography (PET) scan and a magnetic resonance imaging (MRI), to be sure there were no head injuries. The hammering of the MRI machine made me want to go into another altered state of consciousness, but I wasn't up to it. That's when I began to wonder if I might be able to change my reality whenever I chose.

After a day of eating regular food, the I.V. tube was removed from the vein in my arm. I got to take a shower while the nurse stood outside the shower stall in case I felt dizzy. That was the best shower I ever had. I rubbed the shampoo into my long, thick hair, rinsed it out, repeated the shampooing a second time and applied a conditioner. The yellow dye from where I'd had antiseptic fluids swabbed on my scratches and bumps began to disappear under the warm water. The hospital emergency room doctors had put several stitches in the deep cut on my knee, but the nurse said it had healed enough and it wouldn't hurt anything if it got wet. That scar on my knee remains a visible reminder of the day I almost drowned. The shower was absolutely luxurious. I really wanted to stay in longer, but I knew the nurse had other patients in need of her attention. My bruises still showed, even through my dark skin. The sudden energy from the shower quickly gave way to another round of fatigue, and I went back to bed and slept all afternoon.

When the time came to leave the hospital, I got dressed with a little help from my mother. She had brought me sweatpants and a loose top to wear home. The nurse directed me into a wheelchair for the trip to the car. I felt a bit silly and conspicuous in that wheelchair. One of the medical staff had said, "No point in tiring yourself out before you get home." My father said, "Be prepared to see a large group of people outside the room who want to take your picture." As the door to the hospital room opened, I became aware of a lot of noisy activity in the hall. Some photographers asked if I could pose for just one picture. My father agreed to just one, and about a million flashes went off. Now I understood why

I'd been wheeled down to have the CAT scan and MRI during the night. Those reporters and photographers had been spending their days outside my room waiting to get a picture ever since I arrived, leaving only when visiting hours were over. A few asked me how I was feeling, and I said I was glad to be going home. My family and the staff circled around the wheelchair to protect me from the prying eyes and cameras of the press. The press followed us all the way to the parking garage. I hugged and thanked all the staff who had taken care of me and got into our car.

The hour-long ride home from the hospital began. I couldn't remember ever feeling so grateful to be going home. Light rain was falling, bringing new life to the planet, and I felt like I was returning to the planet with my new life. Our symbiotic relationship was going to continue, because for some reason my life had been spared yet again. Now all I needed to do was discover why and what I was supposed to do for the rest of it.

When we arrived home, a few local press people were at the house. My father asked them to please respect our privacy, and to their credit, they began to leave. Before they pulled away, they managed to take a picture of me walking toward the house, which was in the next day's newspaper. I wanted more than anything to see Aussie and Cascade and our house. It felt so good just to walk

through the front door. I had to sit down in the living room for awhile before I had the strength to walk upstairs to my room. My mother brought me a cup of home-made chicken soup that a neighbor had brought over. My appetite had returned. Now I could enjoy food again. Aussie put his head in my lap and Cascade started licking my legs, something she had never done before. I wondered if that was her way of kissing me. Both of my

hands got quite a petting workout that afternoon. It was at least another week before I began to feel like myself. The ordeal had taken more out of me than I had realized. During that week I began to look at the baskets of fruit, gifts and cards that had begun arriving. Friends and many of the survivors of the boating accident had written cards and letters. My mother, always the efficient one, kept a list of everything that came in the door. My father handled all the press calls. His response was always, "We appreciate your call, but no, nobody in the family is granting any interviews at this time. We thank you for your concern." The list of gifts, the log of the telephone calls from family members and friends and the newspaper clippings about the accident were placed in a large white three-ring binder. I talked briefly with my Canadian relatives who had seen the news on their Canadian Broadcasting Corporation (CBC) television. My mother had kept them informed about my recovery. I hadn't realized we knew so many people until I looked at the list and comments of everyone who called.

Kilmer stuck pretty close to me the first weeks after I came home from the hospital. I could tell she was trying not to baby me or let me think she was worried about me. Teenagers think it's not cool to let tender feelings show, but several times she climbed on top of the bed with me and we talked. We didn't talk about the boating accident, but about silly things, like when school was starting, who we thought our teachers would be and what new clothes we should buy. We discussed the school track team. She wanted me to join the team now that I would be a freshman. I wondered if I would be able to run as fast as my animal spirits in a competition. Sometimes she read to me. Her voice relaxed me and sometimes put me to sleep. Each day I tried to spend more time in the living room and yard than in bed. Kilmer and I started taking walks around the neighborhood every day, each day extending the length a little.

As soon as I was up for it, I went to the meditation circle in our back yard for a visit with the animals on our totem pole. The wolf seemed to have changed slightly in appearance. He still looked like a wolf, but I could also see the face of the dog that had helped rescue me from the Chesapeake Bay. As I stared at it, the face seemed to take turns looking back—first the wolf and then the dog. I dropped to my knees, held my arms up to the wolf dog and gave thanks to him for saving my life. The fish and the bird still looked out at the world, watchful as they had always been. I hadn't actually seen them while I was in the water. I only felt them around me. I also gave thanks to the fish and the bird for their help. The two human spirits at the top of the totem pole continued their vigil as well. It was good to have their spirits watching out for me again. I was beginning to really enjoy this new experience of communicating "telepathically" with my animal friends. As I always did whenever I walked into the meditation circle, I touched the "hand of fate" to receive its continuing energy and blessings. I even got a welcome home rattle from the snakeskin that had materialized from under our meditation rock and was now wrapped around the "hand of fate."

(See APPENDIX to Chapter 13 at back of book to learn more about Oglala Sioux shaman Black Elk's explanation on the meaning of circles.)

One day Kilmer gently asked, "Do you think we could discuss some of your healing books?" We began reading and discussing them together. I was pleased that she showed so much interest. We hadn't talked about it previously, but she confessed that she had wanted to discuss the power of healing. Before long, we were discussing everything about my dreams and the different levels of consciousness. I discovered that she also had vivid dreams and had been trying to interpret them or associate them with her waking life. After awhile, we began discussing ways to change our realities, and she began journeying to the spirit world with me. Once I taught her how to do it, she was eager to continue the process.

I shared with Kilmer how my shamanic journeys took me to three different worlds. I began each journey by turning on my drumming tape. I would fly from the top of a tree to reach the upper world, and as soon as I got above the clouds, I could see lots of bright lights. The middle world is similar to our normal reality, but often contains past histories, which I accessed for whatever the journeying purpose happened to be. Sometimes I traveled to the middle world for nothing more than centering and a conversation with the spirits and my power animals. Through a tree trunk I entered the lower world to forests, caves, seas and jungles. The spirits and animals are often nonordinary beings in the lower world. I never ceased to be amazed at how far I could travel in ten to fifteen minutes before the drumming brought me back. I learned that shamanic practitioners come to understand that we live in an unlimited universe. There's real time and then there's shamanic time. We learn how "unimportant is the importance of our time."

The first joint journey Kilmer and I took bound us together forever. I started the drumming tape and told Kilmer, "When the drumming cadence changes after ten or fifteen minutes, we will return to our current reality. Your job during your journey is to visualize a starting place and travel to the world of your choice: lower, middle or upper. Wait for your power animal to be revealed." She said, "I'll fly out this window and go to the upper world for my first try, if that will work." I decided to journey in the middle world, which I entered by going through the back door of our house. My journey took me to a favorite tree in Rock Creek Park, and I climbed to the top of it. I could see Kilmer and her power animal, which turned out to be a lioness with a full and beautiful mane, up above. They were somewhere in Africa, and the lioness was protecting her from a wild herd of zebras. Kilmer could run as fast as the lioness. They darted from boulder to tree to the ground and back to the boulder. My last vision of her and her power animal was seeing them go behind a boulder. When the drumming tape changed cadence and signaled our call to return to our reality, we opened our eyes. In an excited voice, she said, "I could see your face through the leaves of a tree while I was traveling with my power animal!" I responded, "And I watched you both during my own journey from the top of a tree!" Then we both started laughing.

In a later journey, Kilmer's teacher revealed himself to her. It was her father, Keon, and thereafter he played a protective role during her journeys. I figured he had always been protective of Kilmer even though she didn't remember him and couldn't "see" him until now. Now she could see him during her meditative journeys. Kilmer said, "Having my father with me again gives a whole new meaning to the phrase, 'being with you in spirit.'" She told her mother about her shamanic journeys and seeing her father. She said her mother held her tight and began swaying at the revelation while she expressed gratitude to the universe for allowing Kilmer to finally know her wonderful father. Keon had been killed way too soon during his life on earth. His spirit was apparently still around, enjoying contact with his family. The new revelation opened a higher level of communication between Uli and Kilmer about the father Kilmer had not known until now. Kilmer gained other power animals in each world. They helped her at different times, depending on her needs of the moment.

Three months later my parents, Uli and Kilmer, Frank and Jane and I met the high school students and chaperones who were on the boat that flipped over on the Chesapeake Bay. We had corresponded briefly with get-well wishes and thank you notes for their cards and gifts. We had been invited to a Sunday afternoon celebration at their church. The first thing I noticed after we arrived was someone filming the whole affair. All of them had recovered from the bumps and bruises of the impact when the boat overturned, except for one. Abbe, the minister's wife, had been the most severely injured when the motorboat had landed on top of her. She was walking with crutches and gave me a warm hug as she introduced herself. She said, "Despite my unconscious state while awaiting rescue, I could feel healing hands guiding me through the water toward the sailboat. I kept hearing your voice and an older man's voice. I assumed he was your guardian angel hovering above. You were both telling me not to give up. I knew then that I would somehow survive." I hardly knew what to say as I realized that she had also experienced my teacher-grandfather's presence. I wondered if anyone else had seen him.

Abbe said, "My goal has been to recover in time to play the organ this afternoon, and I think I've reached it." She had been in rehabilitative therapy almost daily since the accident. We were about to discover that she was quite a talented organist.

After the initial get-acquainted session in the hall separating the church from the school, we went into the sanctuary and were treated to the most beautiful singing and organ playing I'd ever heard. Rev. Hutton delivered an inspiring sermon about the importance of dealing with what life sends our way and yet keeping the faith that there is a higher purpose to our lives than the present happenings.

Thereafter the church held a celebration of rebirth on the anniversary of the crash. It became a yearly event, and I have been able to join them for most of the celebrations. I correspond with many of them to this day. Their survival became part of the foundation for my spiritual work as I became more aware of the fragility of our life on this planet and the need to use it wisely and well. Our physical bodies would come and go, but our spiritual bodies lived forever. It is important to attend to the spiritual part of ourselves.

Later that summer, I began thinking about how I could change my reality and began to practice changing it. Possessing that kind of power presented a bit of an unsettling prospect for me, but I couldn't seem to resist experimenting. Sometimes I would concentrate hard to get to a meditative state, and without the benefit of the drumming tape my spiritual body would take off through the front door. I entered the lower world through a hollow tree trunk, and wherever it landed me was the world I would be in. Spirit would take me wherever I was supposed to go in that world. If I wanted to go to the upper world, I flew out the window of my room and soared above the treetops. Soon I would be floating in a new world up there. Still other times my spiritual body ran out the back door or through the window of my room and stayed in the middle world, except that it wasn't anything like what was surrounding me. I was immediately someplace else, like on a lake, at the top of a mountain, or sitting in a pasture with domesticated animals around me. I never knew where the spirit would take me. Fortunately, Kilmer was right there with me as we continued our journeys to the spirit world and experienced other levels of consciousness. Our inside joke was to promise each other that neither would ever get lost on our journeys and that we would always return safely.

Toward the end of that summer, things had returned to normal. Or so I thought. Things would never be normal for me again. My survival raised another whole set of issues. I wanted to figure out what had happened during the hours I was in the water. But how could I figure it out if I couldn't remember most of what happened? Had part of my life been left in the water? Did I have more control over my life and the elements than I previously realized? How could I have possibly saved myself from drowning without some outside help or divine intervention of some sort? Was there more to the story of my life being saved than the role of my animal friends on our totem pole? I was feeling pretty strong again, but wondered if things would become more clear once my physical strength and energy returned to its former level.

Chapter Fourteen
Can I Still Become a Shaman after a Television Interview?

Part of our family's Sunday morning ritual was watching the CBS Sunday Morning television show while we read the newspapers and ate a leisurely breakfast. Several months after the boating accident, we received a call from **Charles Osgood**, the host of the show. He asked if he could interview my parents and me and the rest of the sailboat crew about how our lives had changed since the accident. To my surprise, everyone agreed to talk with him. I was a bit hesitant but agreed to go if everyone else did. The interview would be held in the CBS studio in downtown Washington, D.C. Like most teenagers, I was self-conscious about my appearance. After about a half-dozen attempts, I settled for a red and white striped blouse and blue jeans for the interview. I must have been feeling patriotic. The worst part of the interview was having thick makeup put on my face. I hated it because I broke out with acne whenever I put anything except medicated cream on my face. I couldn't wait to get that nasty stuff washed off.

The interview was low-key, and I answered Mr. Osgood's questions about the three of us circling around the passengers and helping them get to the sailboat. Most of the questions centered on the rescue of the passengers and whether we had noticed any changes in our lives. The rest of the group answered those queries. Kilmer was very poised as she related her memories of the day. "After diving into the water to help passengers move toward the sailboat, I quickly realized I was having difficulty breathing, despite the fact that I'm a runner. Somehow I was able to conquer my fears so I could continue to help rescue the passengers, and, fortunately, everyone in the water was rescued. I was quite impressed with how everyone associated with the rescue and hospital stay were so solicitous of us. I'm glad to have my best friend War-ne-la still around so we can finish growing up together. In fact, after the accident, I decided we should stop any quarrelling between us. I don't want to have any regrets if anything were to happen to either of us. Besides, I feel War-ne-la is now grown up enough that we can have a mature friendship."

After the camera stopped focusing on Kilmer, she stuck her tongue out and made a face at me, which I returned. Stern looks from both of our mothers immediately stifled our misbehavior. No more quarrelling? Are you kidding? That'll be the day!

Frank said, "I've thought several times how curious it was that our sailboat happened to be at the scene and how gratifying it was to help save so many lives. Maybe that's why we chose *Survivor* for the sailboat's name." Jane, Uli and my mother talked about how they kept reassuring everyone bobbing about in the water to stay calm while Kilmer, my father and I helped them over to the boat's transom to be pulled aboard.

My mother swallowed hard a few times but kept her composure as she related how hard it was to concentrate on soothing others when she didn't know where her own child was. My mother said that once I jumped off the sailboat, she had a premonition that she wouldn't be seeing me again for awhile.

My father, in a softer than usual voice, said, "We were in despair at not being able to find War-ne-la in the water near the rescue site. Searching for her was one of the longest days of our lives, knowing that every hour that passed lessened hopes that she would be found alive. We felt such overwhelming gratitude when we saw her head lift up from the sand as we were running toward the place where she had crawled ashore."

Uli, in her beautiful African accent, said "I had become aware some time ago that War-ne-la was going to be in danger. So I did the only thing I could—I prayed to my ancestral spirits that she might be spared from an early death." Uli relayed the legend behind the blue mask of her tribe that was identical to what happened that day on the Chesapeake Bay. It was the same blue mask that always communicated with me whenever I visited Uli and Kilmer. Its spirit had always told me he would be seeing me again. Uli said the spirit within the mask had intervened to save me from drowning. Once again, Uli was participating in one of the ancient legends of her people. She had yelled to Kilmer as she dove off the sailboat to watch after me.

During the summer after the rescue of the passengers, Kilmer said, "You know, I felt guilty when they couldn't find you in the water. I thought it was because I had not heeded my mother's admonition to look out for you." I told her, "You shouldn't feel bad. There was just too much to think about on that day, and you couldn't be expected to help save the lives of 14 people and be responsible for me as well." I also told her, "You deserve a lot of credit for keeping your head and helping save so many people. What happened to me was in no way a negative reflection on you." She hugged me when I told her that.

During the television interview, everyone mentioned their renewed appreciation for the gift of life and their realization of how quickly it can end. I had been so focused on my own survival and recovery that I had not thought much about how the incident had affected the others. I didn't get asked what I thought might have happened during the hours before I made it to shore and was rescued. That was probably just as well, because I was still figuring it out. The only time Mr. Osgood came close to that part of the story was when he asked, "And you, War-ne-la, any quarrel with how the day turned out?" I managed to mutter a "none at all" response.

After the interview was over, the CBS crew handed out gifts to each of us. Charles Osgood took me aside and handed me a wrapped package. He said, "I'm proud of you and want to give you something special for helping to save so many lives." I didn't quite know how to respond. I had not thought of myself as having done anything that anyone else would not have done under the same circumstances. He gave me that big smile of his, put his hand on my shoulder, and said, "I would like for us to stay in touch with each other. We both enjoy playing the piano, so perhaps the next time we could play something together. I have the sense that your life has been spared so you can go on to do other great things, and I want to hear about them." I responded, "Thank you, Mr. Osgood, for this gift and for interviewing us." Mr. Osgood had a lot of energy around him. It was a surprise to me that television stations would give gifts to people they interviewed. I wondered how they would know what to select.

Each of the gifts represented something special. Mine was a miniature crystal medicine wheel and a card that said "Thank You" and was signed "Charles Osgood and the CBS Sunday Morning Television Crew." Mr. Osgood had included two of his business cards in the envelope.

I had only a minimal understanding from reading my healing books of what a medicine wheel represented. I knew that it symbolized a person's circle of power, knowledge and understanding, and that it was used to teach the balance and relationship of all things. Once again the circle of life had vividly presented itself to me.

I could only imagine the ancient peoples viewing their world in terms of circles and cycles, and time as circular rather than linear. Medicine wheels taught how the natural order of things work, the human's place in that order, and the purpose of life. They also showed the powers that hold the universe in balance. As I learned more about my medicine wheel, I realized that it could change and adapt to people in their present time circumstances. The medicine wheel is meant to stimulate your thoughts, intuition, seeing and feeling processes, and to move you closer to your own spirit. I would have lots of hours ahead of me to study the medicine wheel and its role in my development. The more I studied, the more insistent the spirits were, calling to me every day. From the stained-glass window and circle dance at the church where my cousin Nidra's wedding took place, to our back yard meditation circle to Black Elk's circle story, to my new medicine wheel, circles seemed to be a recurring theme in my life. I rather liked the whole concept.

We were mailed a videotape of the television interview shown to the rest of the world, and I've watched it numerous times since then. There was no film of the actual crash, so that was shown through animation, based on numerous eye-witness accounts of the accident. A crew member on another boat had recorded the audio portion of the rescue activities on the water that day, but the quality wasn't very good because of the interference of the weather sounds and the human voices. The video portion was almost worthless too because of the sudden darkness and the rocking of the boat. The television crew had listened to the tape and used it to help with the sequence of the events that took place that day. The interview was interspersed with the animated portion. That must be what studio employees do in their editing rooms. The process of putting the piece together was fascinating to me. There was a surprise addition at the end of the film. The studio had included the film of the church group during their choir performance. In the hall of their church, several of the survivors had talked to Charles Osgood about their rescue experiences. It was interesting to hear their perspectives on the rescue and being saved from drowning. All of us had plenty of time to relive the feelings of possibly drowning following a freak accident. I was glad the CBS Sunday Morning show had included as part of the broadcast the young people, their chaperones and their choir singing in their church. They had displayed a great deal of courage while facing possible drowning, and the television station paid tribute to their steadfastness and faith by broadcasting their interviews.

I have trouble believing that the thirteen-year-old girl on the television screen is really me. That was before I became aware of something called sexuality. That was before I understood how to keep what I was thinking and feeling from showing on my face. That was before I learned that some people wanted to become friends because I'd been on television. That was before I learned that boys were interested in something other than the conversation at hand. That was before I learned that schools and universities could not teach me all that I needed to know to fulfill my life's prophecy. That was before I understood how to use the powers I had been given to first heal myself, and then to heal others. The most significant part of my own healing took place during my shamanic journeys. I kept getting stronger and stronger every day. The spirits were constantly with me now.

So that's the way I began learning how to put the ancient practice of shamanistic healing to use. The journeys to the spirit world to learn the skills needed for my life's calling were filled with absolute wonder. My teacher-grandfather often appeared during my journeys. My totem animal helpers turned out to be a camel and a white wolf. They appeared and offered themselves to me during the time I was ill in the hospital in Central America. The camel's name is Dust and the white wolf's name is Snow. Snow came to me as an orphaned pup, and I became her surrogate parent. She grew to adulthood quickly, after which our roles reversed and she became my protector. She must have been a distant cousin to the black wolf on our totem pole. Later on, butterflies, honey bees, a hawk, a seal and a grizzly bear joined the power animal menagerie. My life as a shaman was just beginning.

I began my worldwide travels to study with other shamans. For my birthday that year, my parents gave me the most treasured gift I've ever received, and it has remained near my side ever since the day it was unwrapped. Inside its own carrying case was a Kwakiutl handmade drum covered with elk skin and a drum beater stick. The beating end of the stick was covered in deer skin, and the other end had beaver teeth marks where it had been separated from its limb. I wondered if that beaver knew his hard work chomping that branch away from its limb would create a drum beater stick held in my hand for many years to come. I wanted to believe he left it for me personally. The bark had been left on the stick where my hand grasped it, which made for good traction as I held it. From that day on, I continued beating my drum nearly every day for ten to twenty minutes. That's how I have stayed connected with Mother Earth and what has kept me grounded to her heartbeat. Mother Earth would stay inside me during my entire life.

The maker of the Kwakiutl drum had enclosed a note suggesting the recipient take a journey to the spirit of the drum. A few days after I settled down from the initial excitement of having my very own drum and stick, I sat in my room preparing for a journey to the spirit of this drum. I turned on the drumming tape and rubbed my hands all over my new drum. I felt myself spiraling into the drum itself. My journey began in the middle world as I ventured forth to meet the spirit of my drum. My body continued the spiral dance before stopping at the water's edge of a rocky coastline. The rocks were tall and thick and the ocean waves were slamming into them pretty hard, creating huge sprays of water with each arrival. I watched the waves and rocks for awhile. Suddenly, from behind the rocks, a seal appeared. She kept nodding her head up and down toward me and communicated that she had come to look after me and my drum. My drum's spirit was a seal? I hadn't expected anything like that, but then I realized I hadn't really known what to expect. In fact, I never knew what to expect on my shamanic journeys. Maybe the day would arrive when I would no longer be surprised at what was revealed on those journeys. So now I had another power animal protecting me. With the seal inhabiting my drum, she would always be nearby in case any need for her protection arose. There was no doubt in my mind that I would be utilizing her at some point in the future.

I carried the drum and case on one shoulder and my backpack on the other whenever I traveled. The inside of the drum was a perfect place to carry the other tools for my training—incense, candles, smudge pot, bones, feathers, tobacco, crystals, sage and other herbs, along with the ever-present current journal. Everything had its own sealable plastic bag. I quickly learned to remove any tobacco, herbs and matches if I was flying someplace. The airport security screeners became a little too curious, so I continually changed the contents of my bag of tools, depending on the occasion. It was a good thing I had a strong back and shoulders. Otherwise, I could never carry everything with me. When Kilmer was available, she traveled with me. Once she entered college, she could only travel with me during the summers when she wasn't working.

Uli and Kilmer played a huge role in my later development. Our trip to Africa the summer after Kilmer graduated from college was their first opportunity to check on the remaining members of their family. Their family welcomed me as one of their own, and I eagerly returned their affection. Their tribal society had much to teach me, and I soaked up their wisdom the entire time we were there. But that's another whole story.

Some days my mind would journey willingly to the spirit world. Some days I would resist its pull. There were times when I found myself in the spirit world when I had not consciously done a thing to get there. My spirit's strong call continued. Once I realized there was no other way to satisfy my curiosity and fascination with the spirits, my desire to escape their attraction went away. I wanted to find out what the spirit world held, to work with my power animals and teachers, and to go wherever that spirit world would take me. I wanted to harness this new empowerment to make the world a better place. I decided to start modestly with healing everything in my little piece of the world. The universe and the spirits had a lot to teach me about my adolescent idealism. It took a long time for me to realize how much bigger the world was than everything I knew or had experienced. I was but a cog in a far greater plan. But what a plan it was!

All that journeying to the spirit world nearly wore out the drumming tape that Uli had given me. My brain waves synchronized with the drumbeat as I went into a totally different reality. It was totally different from the dreaming reality and from the reality of my room. After the ten to fifteen minutes of the journey transpired and the drumming tempo changed, I returned from the spirit world to the present reality. To help me remember and keep track of what I experienced in the spirit world, I recorded whatever transpired during my journeys in my journals. I have continued writing down those experiences and still do it after every journey. I'm afraid my bookcases have become rather crowded.

Once I began the nightly journeying ritual, I knew there would be no stepping away from quenching my thirst for discovery and learning. I had to fulfill my spiritual vision quest. I just had to. The only question remaining was whether I could become a real shaman in today's society.

Chapter Fifteen
Spiritual Vision Quest in the Blue Ridge Mountains

I did go on a spiritual vision quest to be sure I was on the right path toward fulfilling my destiny. It was as though I somehow needed confirmation that shamanism was to be my true calling. I needed to find out if I was ready to surrender myself to a Higher Wisdom and receive my life's mission, that is, if it was to be given to me. The native tribes of long ago often went out into the desert or mountains for three or four days and nights, fasting before and during the quest. My parents and I agreed that it would be better to begin just before dawn, rather than spend the night outdoors by myself in unfamiliar terrain, at least for the first night. After several discussions, we decided to travel to the Shenandoah Valley of Virginia and see if the Blue Ridge Mountains would be conducive to my quest. We stayed in a cabin, and I let myself out of the room well before dawn and began my trek up the mountain, carrying water and my shaman materials. I had not eaten anything the day before and would eat nothing this day. Nor did I drink from my water bottle.

My eyes adjusted quickly to the dark, and with the help of a waning moon I was able to see without using a flashlight. A small owl was flying in front of me, seeming to lead me upwards. That seemed like a good metaphor of wisdom for the beginning of my quest. Part of the way up the path of the mountain, I began softly using my rattle. When my rattle stopped making any noise despite my soft shaking, I knew I had arrived at the place where I was supposed to be. I smudged myself with sage and made a circle around me. I thanked all the elements around me—the trees, rocks, plants, animals and insects— for being there with me, and I invited them to help me with my quest.

I sat down and wrapped the blanket around me. I waited for the sun to rise, and as usual, it didn't disappoint me. I hadn't realized how far I had walked up the mountain. It was comforting to feel close to the Creator. It seemed like I could see forever into the vast distances below. I sat looking out at the landscape and listening for the sounds and the feel of nature. My task was to be alert to everything going on around me. I sat for only a short while when a hawk suddenly soared above me, shrieking out

I could see his beak opening and closing each time his shrill cry cut the air. I felt he was beckoning me to join him, but it wasn't clear how I was supposed to do that. Apparently, I was a hard sell, so the hawk flew off, perhaps looking for another approach to reach me. I noted everything

I saw or felt in my journal. My mind kept trying to wander, but I was able to bring my thoughts back to the peaceful surroundings. I continued with mindful breathing for the awareness of my oneness with nature and help in staying on my spiritual path. I tried to stay focused on who I was and why I was here on this earth.

Visions began to creep into my mind. I found myself on a train where the passengers were all the animals I had ever seen, in pictures and in reality. Each car of the train had additional animals. I was dressed in a conductor's navy blue suit, walking through all the railroad cars with a director's baton in my hand. The train stopped, and I led all the animals out of the train and up to the top of a mountain. Each of them sat down, and I began talking with them about what was going on in their worlds. My director's baton was used for emphasis whenever I made a point. The hawk appeared on a tree branch above me. Each time I gestured with the baton, he would shriek. Once the discussion about the state of the earth ended, my animal friends began dancing, and I joined them. Whoever said you couldn't teach an elephant to dance never took a shamanic journey or participated in a vision quest. Actually, it wasn't hard—he kept lowering his trunk for me to hold. We were keeping time to a beating drum, but I have no idea where it was coming from. I wondered if Noah of the Old Testament ever danced with the animals on his ark.

Could the vision mean I was to be a musical conductor, a hostess on a train, or a veterinarian? Only later did I make the analogy to teaching, for we had each been teaching the other about our earth. My teacher-grandfather appeared and spoke about the survival of people on this planet and how that very survival depended on those who have a good connection with the spiritual world. He visited me off and on throughout the day. I began to think of him as my spiritual interpreter or sponsor, in addition to my teacher. I knew logically that he couldn't really be there, but all the same, he was. He talked to me as he always had while I was still a child. After a brief appearance he would say he was leaving me alone with nature and would disappear. I stayed open and waited for whatever might come to fill the void in my stomach and brain.

The hawk returned in my next vision. I knew from my reading that seeing a hawk meant that my ability to see would be sharpened. I could now be encouraged to examine life from a higher perspective. I could be more open to opportunities and any hazards that might block my progress as I continued my life's journey. The hawk began shrieking again, and this time I understood what he was trying to tell me. He told me I could now observe without flinching whatever appeared in front of me, no matter how disgusting or frightening. That removal of fear would enable me to tell the difference between real and imagined danger. I could have sworn the hawk had blue eyes.

The blue haze of the aptly named mountains lifted and the sun shone brightly. Clouds formed into strange shapes. The changing patterns could have been formed by the exhaust of an airplane, but I knew nothing could match the Creator's designs. I became aware of a pattern in the clouds as they engulfed me. First one would lift me up, and then another would descend and carry me back to earth. The process created a roller coaster effect. The pace of the rising and lowering increased, and soon my brain was shaking inside my skull and I began to feel dizzy. I landed on the ground with a thud and immediately tightened the blanket around me, even though the sun was warm. Did that mean I would be an airline pilot or that my life would have so many ups and downs that it would be hard to stay grounded?

Part of my meditations during the day revolved around my feelings about the vision quest and whether I was truly willing to become a shaman. What would it mean for my future if I surrendered to whatever spirit or higher power was calling me toward the life of a healer? Would this vision quest have the same result as the ones of old that took place in the deserts? When the ones of old were led to go on a vision quest and passed whatever test or tests were presented, they returned and became healers. All those I had studied experienced that transformation upon their return. Maybe some went on vision quests and came back unchanged. But then, they probably never told anyone about their experiences for fear of sounding like they had failed in their life's mission. It felt good to be able to think so clearly while surrounded with only my spirits keeping me company.

The Blue Ridge Mountains are filled with deer. Because they have little fear of being hunted in a national forest, they have become gentle and almost tame. There was a small grassy area off to the side of where I was, and during that day it was frequented by numerous deer. The small herd had lots of new fawns, still with their spots. I loved watching them nurse from their mothers. Whenever they heard a sound, they would stop nursing and look around, the milk still on their lips. At one point I realized the entire area was filled with fawns, and no adults were left to watch over them. The nursery had been left unguarded. I walked over to where they were and sat in the grass with them. Many of them nuzzled me. Without any warning, a coyote appeared on the cliff. Rather than

scatter in search of their parents, the fawns all stood around me. As soon as the coyote saw me, he shrank away and walked back down the mountain. While part of me wished that all animals could live in peaceful harmony, the other part knew that this coyote was looking for a meal, and I didn't want it to be any of the fawns who had been mysteriously left in my care. Did this vision mean I was supposed to be a wildlife protector or a nanny in a nursery school? All these visions were confusing me, but I kept writing the experiences down in my journal.

My last vision of that day had to do with bees. The apple orchard farmers of the Shenandoah Valley depend on honey bees to pollinate the apple blossoms. They were swarming around me, and the buzz began to take the form of conversation. I was being told that their hives were being invaded by enemy forces. They were asking for help before all of them died. As quickly as they appeared, they left. My mind went immediately to the story Anton Chekhov wrote about beehives. I wasn't sure what this vision meant, but I did learn later that indeed a mite had infested the honey bee larvae and was in fact destroying the population. At one point, the apple orchard farmers had to import hives of bees from other states. Was I supposed to be an entomologist who could forecast the danger a stressed insect population might harbinger for the rest of the planet?

The sunset that day was the most beautiful I had ever seen. I felt as one with the Creator, being allowed to participate in yet another of nature's awesome happenings. I thought about how often most of us take such wondrous experiences for granted. Once the sun went below the horizon, I walked back down the mountain so as not to worry my parents. Had I become too civilized to truly benefit from a vision quest?   I would have to see what tomorrow brought. I did not eat that evening but did share the cabin with my parents another night.

On the second day I again left the cabin early in the morning. Only this time, I went to a completely different spot. The sun was rising and showing itself occasionally through thick black clouds. The spot I located was under a cliff overhang. It was a good choice because the heavens emptied themselves of rain off and on during the day. Lightning and the ensuing thunder accompanied the showers. I wondered if I should interpret the thunder as the Creator's way of talking to me and the lightning as the Creator's way of showing me the earth and heavens more clearly. I studied the storm intently, staying very still so I could be open to any visions. I could feel my teacher-grandfather's presence under the overhang. Pretty soon the lightning was making patterns in the sky. It looked like caribou running across the sky. I wondered if this vision suggested wildlife protection, just as one of yesterday's visions had. Or could it mean I was to travel north where the caribou lived?

Once the rain ended, there was new forestation around me I had not noticed before the rain began. The small trees were bending slightly in the breeze, showing off their beauty. They beckoned me to hold onto them as a brace against the wind. I walked as the spirits commanded, through the small trees toward the edge of the cliff. There was nothing to hold me on the cliff. I didn't fall but simply began flying with the hawk as my companion and guide. This was my first shapeshifting experience, as I took on the hawk's characteristics and talents. There was nobody to call to because there was nobody around to hear me. We continued flying around the mountains. My vision became that of a hawk, seeing every little thing that moved, including rabbits and mice. Where was the hawk taking me? Did this vision mean that I was to look at the big picture of life and at the same time notice all the smaller details? The hawk finally escorted me back to my place, and when my eyes opened, I was seated safely on the blanket again.

Butterflies began lighting on the blossoms of the new trees. I knew from the many butterflies that visited Rock Creek Park that they were able to dispel negative energy. Butterflies transform themselves from an egg to a larva to a caterpillar to a cocoon and then to a flying insect. While writing the experience of the butterflies in my journal I realized the metaphor of transformation in the continuous process of development and spiritual evolution. Could the butterflies help in my transformation to shamanic work? The first issue in any transformation would be leaving my old self behind, as the butterfly left its cocoon behind. If I didn't leave some of the old stuff behind, there would be no room for new experiences. Could the butterflies give me the courage to launch new wings and face new challenges? If that was what the butterflies were suggesting, I would have to wait a few years to find out if the interpretation of the butterflies was going to become fact. As a fourteen-year-old, I couldn't begin to live on my own.

In walking away from my place under the cliff overhang for a few minutes, some force drew me to a rose quartz rock that had been split in two. The outside of both pieces had been worn smooth by the wind and rain and were faded in color. The inside of the split rock was jagged and deep rose in color. The quartz was reflecting the sun's rays in brilliant lights. Quartz crystals are sometimes called *stars within the earth*. That's exactly how the rock looked to me. I could not take my eyes off the split rock and its shimmering. It may not have been alive, but it was filled with some kind of energy.

I had studied quartz crystals and how shamans use them to "see" the spirits or a patient's soul. They're used as links or bridges between the inner world of the spirit and the outer material world that we know as current reality. Shamans use crystals to reflect into being something that was previously only a potential idea. Crystals can also receive, store and transmit light. They can become our allies for self-transformation by helping us discover our inner light that connects us with the light of the Creator.

I remembered learning in my first computer class that quartz crystals are used in building computers because of their electronic and electrical properties. The atoms in a crystal are arranged in precise patterns and are held accurately in place by enormous energies. These atoms attract and magnetize vibrations. Anyone who has worked with crystals will tell you that they feel uplifted and energized, and their extrasensory perception is greatly enhanced. One of the great secrets of the ancient shamans was the knowledge that a current of energy could be set up in a crystal and carried to a required destination simply by the intention of the human will. That meant a crystal could influence vibration and help make the required change.

Knowing that it was illegal to remove anything from a national forest, I reluctantly let the split rose quartz lie where I had first seen it. Imagine my surprise when I emptied my bag after returning home and found both pieces of the rose quartz rock in the bottom of it. I have no idea how the two pieces got from the ground into my bag. Perhaps it somehow transformed itself into something that could move into a bag, or perhaps my unspoken desire for it provided the energy for it to move into my bag. The two pieces of crystal sit on the windowsill of my room where they continue to shimmer in the light of the sun and moon. With my spirit uplifted, possibly from being around the crystals and butterflies, I could hardly sit still to watch the second day's sunset. I could barely see the sun through the hanging clouds. Despite the clouds, it felt like the falling rain had washed any impurities out of the air to provide another peaceful end of a beautiful day. Again I walked down the hill to meet my parents. On the way down the mountainside, a bat flew in front of me. My immediate instinct was of fear and to crouch out of its way. Just as quickly as the instinctive fear arrived, it left. Bats live in caves, symbolic of the womb. They hang upside down, paralleling the unborn self, immersed in darkness. I realized instantly that encountering a bat as I was ending my spiritual vision quest meant that an old way of life was ending and a process of initiation into a new life pattern was beginning. This new bat friend "spirit" would help me face any remaining fears and help me find my way out of darkness into a new understanding of life.

The weekend was nearly over, and we had to return home for the next week's work and school. My parents had spent their time at flea markets, antique stores and farm produce stands. Our car was filled with their two days of acquisitions. With a simple "let's get home" from my father, we headed east.

I wondered if I had adequately and correctly written down all that I had experienced during my two-day vision quest. Perhaps, I thought, I'll go on another one when I have a car and can drive to the mountains or a desert and stay as long as the spirits believe is necessary. For now, I had a lot to reflect upon in respect to what path I had been shown for my adult life. There seemed to be so many possibilities, sort of an embarrassment of riches. I knew to wait and see what appeared before making any decision about turning myself over to the Higher Wisdom. The decision wasn't really mine to make. It had been made a long time ago. I just followed the path set down before me as instructed by the spirits. In one sense, it was the easiest thing I ever did. In another sense, it was the hardest thing I ever had to do. Easy in that I knew it was what I was supposed to do; hard in that nearly every step was filled with uncertainty—not for me, necessarily, but for others. There was never any uncertainty on my part because the spiritual vision quest at the age of fourteen led me to the right choice. Others had to be constantly reassured that they would remain safe during their journeys to unknown worlds. That was part of my calling as a shaman—to keep others safe.

Chapter Sixteen
A "Walkabout" With Papa in Australia's Great Outback

A most enlightening trip during my fifteenth year was with my father. We spent all winter planning it and had lists all over the house. Our plan was to drive and backpack over the Great Outback of Australia, each of us intending to discover whatever we could about our Aboriginal heritage. We would be gone for six weeks during summer in Washington and winter in the "land down under." That was a good time to travel, because the heat might have been unbearable during an Australian summer. Our trip through the Aboriginal lands of the Great Outback, called a "walkabout" by the natives, was mostly motorized, except for the times we backpacked up mountainsides and down to stream beds. My father rented an OKA, which is a vehicle manufactured in Western Australia, so we could cover as much of the country as possible. An OKA is similar to a large four-wheel-drive Jeep or recreational vehicle, made to withstand the rugged terrain of the Great Outback. My father taught me the basics of driving it in the event of an emergency. Wise and precautionary, my father somehow had known I would have to put that knowledge to the test during our trip.

After our arrival in Melbourne, and before leaving for the Outback, we again toured the family vineyards in the southeastern part of the country. Our custom was to visit the gravesites of my grandparents anytime we visited Australia. My father always bought two dried-flower arrangements—roses for my grandmother and eucalyptus for my grandfather. He said those had been their favorite bouquets during their lifetimes. We asked them to keep us safe during our trip. We then headed in a northwesterly direction toward the middle part of the continent. The small towns began thinning out as we headed into desert country. Our first major destination was Uluru, the enormous red rock that is featured in every story of Australia.

Our routine was to pack enough food, water and supplies into the OKA to last a little over a week. We also slept in the OKA. My father would park it in whatever shade he could locate, usually under a eucalyptus tree known as a coolibah. We'd strap on our backpacks and off we'd hike in various directions, returning to the OKA several times a day. My father asked, "Do I look like a swagman carrying my matilda?" The swagmen or vagabonds of old who traveled across Australia carried their bags, or swags, loosely translated to mean they were carrying a bag which provided them whatever they needed, just like a wife with the name of Matilda. They also carried their billy with them, which was a tin can of tea. That legend gave rise to Australia's unofficial national anthem,

"Waltzing Matilda." I realized it was actually a sad song, once I understood all the Australian terms used in the lyrics.

Whenever we came to a town or city, about once a week, we e-mailed greetings from a library or hotel computer to my mother, Uli and Kilmer. We felt the need to stay in touch with home. By the end of each week, we were also ready for a shower, an opportunity to wash our clothes, savor a meal in a restaurant, and sleep indoors in a bed.

After a night's rest in real beds, we would repack the OKA and take off for another week to see more of the Great Outback. I couldn't wait to get started each morning. I'd never been able to get this much time alone with my father. We turned out to be great traveling companions, always looking out for each other. The Great Outback had many dangerous and poisonous creatures, so we had to be vigilant at all times. Our relationship was entering a new phase—searching for our roots.

The Aborigines had arrived about 50,000 years ago from Asia and Indonesia. It was one of history's great migrations over land bridges that no longer exist and took place when the earth was much cooler and the seas were lower. The journeys of the Spirit Ancestors across the land are recorded in Dreaming Tracks and Songlines. Dreaming Tracks were recreated by Aborigines drawing a line representing a stage in their ancestors' journey, interspersed with circles, which represented the scarce waterholes. Songlines were the principal medium of exchange among the natives and represented something of a totemic or emblematic geography. The natives moved from place to place during droughts and fires in order to survive. Songlines helped them mark and find their way through all the territories. Songlines represented some sort of telepathic ability to communicate throughout the ages for both the living and the dead. It was not unusual for Aborigines to suddenly burst into song when they got to a certain place. Each clan or tribe had its own language, rituals and social life. They lived off the bounty of the land, called "bush tucker" by the Europeans. It has been estimated that the Aborigines numbered about one million when the Europeans arrived in 1788. There are only about 275,000 now, or roughly 2 percent of the total Australian population. Most live in urban and rural communities. About

15 percent still live in the Outback, or The Bush. We needed to go where they were. One of my father's objectives was to find out if the Land Rights Act passed by the Australian legislature was living up to its intended purpose – allowing the Aborigines to go back to their lands and, in the process, ridding themselves of the alcoholism that was plaguing them.

I kept a lookout for kangaroos. There are over fifty kangaroo species, ranging in size from the red, which is about seven feet tall, to the mouse, about two inches tall. We saw some in the distance and some around the watering holes, called "billabongs." I had several books in my backpack on native animals, plants and trees. Whenever we saw something out of the ordinary, I tried to locate it in my books so I could record our sightings correctly. However, I couldn't always find what I thought I saw in the books. My horticultural interest was in the native plants and their uses in healing. I looked for different types of roots, grasses, and leaves that were used for pain relief and sedative and antiseptic purposes.

Sometimes I drew the animals and plants, and I often took pictures whenever I could point and shoot the camera quickly enough to record moving targets. We even found some koala bears in a tree. They were sound asleep and not the least bothered by us. At twilight, we frequently saw dingos, the wild white Australian dogs.

Before we arrived at Uluru, we detoured to visit lands set aside as Aboriginal territories. I tried to figure out who the shaman was in each tribe. In Australia, a native shaman is called a karadji, a wingirin, or a kuldukke, depending on where you are, and is known to have unusual seeing powers into the future and the past. Sometimes I identified who the shaman was right away, and other times I didn't see anyone who seemed to fit the part. It's possible that some tribes no longer have their own shaman. So much of the knowledge about the native healing powers was passed on orally from one generation to the next. That ability to pass down the knowledge was interrupted for several generations when the Europeans arrived, and some may have been lost forever.

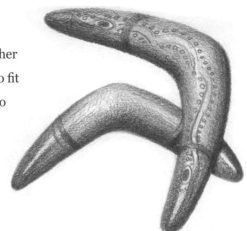

We were almost always met with friendly smiles. I felt that our dark skin identified us as part of them, but I also had the feeling they knew we had native blood in our background. We were usually invited to walk over their lands and sometimes to participate in their healing circles. I had learned before leaving home that the rorē, a sacred crystal, is used in their healing. I had brought lots of crystals with me and always left several with the children of the tribes. We had purchased two dozen boomerangs before leaving Melbourne, and I let the children of each village "teach" me how to throw it properly so it would return. Before we left each village, I presented the boomerang to the child who had thrown it the least far, telling that child that he or she needed the most practice, and to be sure to let the other children help with the practice. I also left a self-inflating kick ball for the children, which I blew up with a tire pump kept in the OKA .

I loved watching the children smile as they shyly touched my clothes and backpack. I had learned a few Aboriginal words and always said hello and good-bye in their Koori language. Each tribe recited one of their legends before we left. I had to really concentrate hard to remember each one so I could record it in my journal as soon as we returned to the OKA. I particularly enjoyed participating in the dance festivals of celebration, known as corroborees, which were held in the evenings. The corroborees celebrated their survival. Kilmer would have loved participating in their dance festivals.

Access to and ownership of Uluru, known previously as Ayers Rock, has been returned to the Aborigines. It's located near the center of the continent and is about three and one-half miles high and about a five-mile hike around. We spent half a day there. It looked completely different close-up, and it changed constantly as we walked around it. The colors changed from fiery red to mauve to pink to blue, depending on where you were and how the sun reflected off the rock. It was majestic in its serenity and presence. There was no question in my mind as to why it had always held such fascination and reverence for the native Aborigines and why it continues to provide curiosity for visitors. Near Uluru is the Spring of Mutitdjilda, sacred to Wanambi, the Aboriginal name for the rainbow serpent.

The kookaburra birds, members of the kingfisher family, were everywhere. The Aborigines consider them protectors, because they feed on poisonous snakes and vermin. Their call, resembling haunting laughter, often sounds a danger alarm. Aborigines may be closer to nature and animals than any other peoples, save native tribes on other continents. In my desire to increase my senses and understanding of my ancestors and their environment, I kept picking up dirt and rubbing it between my fingers. With each handful of dirt, I felt a strengthening of that connection.

We visited more Aboriginal lands before heading farther west. The Aboriginal shamans use eucalyptus trees as antennas to connect with shamans in different parts of the world. They give and receive messages from their brother and sister shamans all over the world through some sort of unseen stream of energy. After observing the process several times, I began to understand more clearly what "one who knows" means. They could "see" and "hear" things that other humans could not. The spirits were their vehicle for enlightenment. Shamans from all over the world have visited the natives of Australia to learn whatever they can about their ancient ways. My father and I were part of a long line of visitors who had the same purpose in mind. Reading about someone's experience just wasn't the same as observing it firsthand.

We continued our trek farther west, made a large U-turn and headed back east toward Cairns, where we expected to snorkel over the Great Barrier Reef. We didn't have the time available to go all the way to the west coast of Australia and had chosen a more northerly route back across the desert. Every day we continued our walks over the desert, mountains, lake beds and old trails. Awesome forces of nature had been at work creating the unusual geologic formations of the continent. Its raw, ancient landscape varied from rock formations to vast deserts to water holes. It was not unusual to look down into a valley thousands and thousands of feet below.

Each visit with the Aborigines provided more information and education for my shaman training. The shamans seemed to have their work cut out for them as they tried vainly to correct the imbalances that the presence of alcohol, which they call "grog," had created in their existence. Our kinship with our ancestors strengthened with each visit. We visited twenty-two tribes in all. I promised to mail each tribe the story I was writing about our trip once I returned home. Neither my father nor I were sure how many of the Aborigines could read English, but we figured someone in their tribe would be able to read it or find someone from a nearby tribe who could. My mother couldn't believe the amount of postage it took to send copies of the story to them. Developing all the pictures we took also cost a small fortune, but we all agreed that it was important to record this once-in-a-lifetime experience. We filled six albums with pictures.

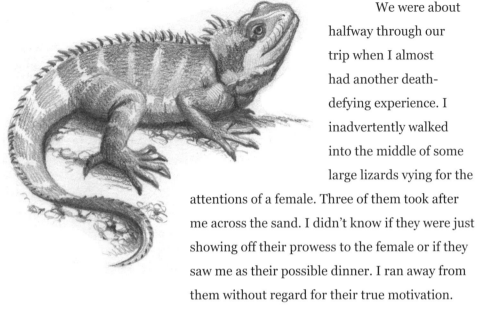

We were about halfway through our trip when I almost had another death-defying experience. I inadvertently walked into the middle of some large lizards vying for the attentions of a female. Three of them took after me across the sand. I didn't know if they were just showing off their prowess to the female or if they saw me as their possible dinner. I ran away from them without regard for their true motivation.

I hadn't realized they could run so fast. It was almost like an old horror movie I had seen on television. My father reacted quickly and yelled, "Circle back to the OKA," as he grabbed a bottle filled with ammonia and water from behind the front seat. I began my wide circle back toward him and the OKA, the lizards nipping at my hiking boots the whole way. My father managed to intercept the chase and spray the lizards with the ammonia water, all the while yelling at them in an effort to distract their attention away from me. Once the liquid hit their eyes, they immediately stopped running because they were temporarily blinded. My father and I took advantage of their confusion and beat a hasty retreat in the OKA. Thanks to my father, I didn't become one of their victims. Once I caught my breath and we were safely away from them, we managed a bit of a laugh. I said, "That wasn't exactly how I wanted to end our trip." We couldn't have known that more danger awaited us.

Through the stories told by the Aboriginal tribes, I discovered what really happened during their native hunting. Without learning how to employ these practices, they would not have survived. They learned through observation and imitation how to mimic with dance and song the animal sounds and movements. Then they used what they had learned as lures and decoys during their hunts. It was a small stretch for the intelligence and senses of the animals to become alive within the consciousness of the hunters. The quarry first becomes part of the hunter in spirit before becoming part of him in flesh. Thus the spirit life of the animal species is extended in exchange for its physical death. Without this mutual giving and receiving, the Aborigines believe that any nourishment from consuming the animals could have destructive effects. I could see how the tribes would never knowingly inflict such bad karma upon themselves.

I had heard stories of how camels had been introduced into Australia for work in the Outback. Their famous ability to endure days of walking without water on the continent of Africa could be expected to serve them equally well in the deserts of Australia. They were still in use at some of the desert settlements. They were also a tourist attraction for rides into the desert. Some had been turned loose or had escaped, surviving in the wild. Occasional sightings of wild herds of camels had been reported. One night in our OKA, we heard but did not see what we thought had to be the sound of camel hooves on the desert floor.

On the northerly route heading back East, around a narrow mountain trail, we unexpectedly came upon some animals drinking water from a pothole in the trail. My father instinctively swerved to keep from hitting them. The OKA tipped over the edge of the road. My last gauge of the distance down the mountain prior to the swerve had seemed a thousand miles. We looked at each other with horrified expressions as the OKA started down the mountain. The scrub trees were banging us around inside the OKA. It was probably only a few seconds, but it seemed like an eternity before the OKA stopped abruptly. We had landed on another narrow trail farther down the mountainside. We were both wearing seatbelts but still managed to bump our heads several times. My father slid the gearshift of the OKA into park and turned the ignition off. He then put his head on the steering wheel. It was a few seconds before I realized that he had passed out. I instantly realized a role reversal in our relationship would have to take place if I were to get us out of our predicament. I had barely begun to react to our situation when my own current level of consciousness left me. My last memory was unbuckling my seat belt, opening the door on my side of the OKA and my feet hitting the ground.

My teacher-grandfather and my wolf power animal, Snow, suddenly arrived on the mountainside. Snow was salivating and licking my face to wake me up. I tried but couldn't. I could feel her hot breath and heard her howl at me. She clawed at my shoulders and chest. I could feel the sharpness of her claws. My teacher-grandfather was trying to open the driver's side door to help my father. It was stuck. My grandfather and Snow dragged my body to the back of the OKA. I must have been lying on the ground a long time. Snow tried periodically to rouse me, but I couldn't seem to wake up. I detested that feeling of helplessness, even if I was unconscious.

A loud clatter of loose rocks falling along the mountainside roused me slightly. Snow began nudging and licking me again. My teacher-grandfather was sitting on the rear bumper of the OKA looking at me. I gradually took in my surroundings as the memory of what had happened with the OKA returned. I wasn't sure I should stand up, so I crawled on my hands and knees to the driver's side of the OKA. The door still wouldn't open, so I managed to get back to the OKA's passenger side and then move my father, still unconscious, into the passenger seat. It took all the strength I could muster to move his "dead" weight across the seat. Now all I had to do was remember what my father had taught me about driving the OKA. I couldn't reach the pedals until I moved the seat closer to the steering wheel. My father remained unconscious in the passenger seat, which I had put into a reclining position.

I turned the key in the ignition and, to my surprise, the motor started. I began slowly guiding the OKA down the rest of the mountainside. I could only hope that someone would find us so we could get help for my father. I periodically took his pulse and found it weakening, and I kept hoping it wouldn't go any lower until I could get us to a place that had a medical facility. My basic training in first aid and CPR was not enough to help him in this state. For the first time since the boating accident at the age of thirteen, I began to feel a sense of foreboding. I had thought I was through with fear, but maybe I had just thought that part of my life was over.

The OKA made it to the bottom of the mountain where the land was flat again and then stopped running. I tried everything I could think of to get it started, but nothing worked. I concentrated hard to keep my wits about me. My father's condition kept me focused on the task at hand. I would have to hike along the road until I located someone, or I could walk to an Aboriginal community. I covered my father with a light blanket and placed a bottle of water near him in case his consciousness returned. I also wrote a big note and left it on the dashboard where he could see it if he awakened. I wrote: "Papa, stay here. I will return with help. I love you, War-ne-la."

I unloaded some of the things from my backpack so it wouldn't be so heavy and added two bottles of water. I reviewed our map and decided I would walk toward a nearby Aboriginal village. I called upon my spirit helpers to give me strength to obtain help for my father. The last thing I remembered was loading my backpack. I collapsed yet again behind the OKA. Would my power animals come through and help us?

My camel power animal, Dust, walked around me as I was lying behind the OKA. After nuzzling my backpack, he began inspecting my shoes. He sat down next to me as if to tell me to hop on his back for a ride. I could barely hold on to his neck as he got up and began walking across the desert. I was vaguely aware that Snow was walking alongside us. I began to hear voices in the distance. An entire tribe of Aborigines met the camel as he deposited me at their feet. I tried to stand and immediately began falling back toward the earth. One of the women and a teenage boy steadied me and helped me walk to a house. They took some water from my backpack and helped me drink it. Though I could speak only a few words of their Koori language and their English was somewhat difficult to interpret, I managed through gestures to communicate that I had left my father back in the desert and that he needed help. Somehow they seemed to understand, and someone brought an old green truck to the front of the house. One woman and the man driving the truck helped me in, and we drove away from their community toward where my father and the OKA were parked. I had acted out the mountainside incident, which may have helped them figure out the location of what I was trying to communicate. They had laid a mattress onto the bed of the truck along with a bag which I assumed contained medicines.

A short distance away from their community, we stopped in front of a spinifex grass hut, known as a worley. A woman, whom I identified immediately as a shaman, was standing between the hut and the road. I guessed from the conversation between her and the passengers of the truck that she had received a message to travel somewhere in a truck. She glanced at me briefly. It was obvious from my traveling shorts and blouse and shoes that I was not native. She had on a faded cotton dress, and her pockets were bulging. She also had an old cloth bag hanging over her shoulder. She rode in the back of the truck on the mattress. I peered at her several times through the back window. She was looking out at the countryside, and I assumed she was seeing things a million miles away.

Upon arrival at the location where the OKA had stopped, their conversation became rapid and intense. My father was coming around and trying to speak. Suddenly, I was lying on the ground and they were gently stroking my face and head and rubbing my arms. The pungent smell of something being held under my nose snapped me awake. How could I still be on the ground near the OKA? Hadn't I just ridden Dust to their community and come back with them in a truck? How could I still be here on the ground? And where were Dust and Snow? If my teacher-grandfather was close by, he would help me. I could hear my father calling me. I managed to stand so I could look things over. The turnabout of events had confused me. It seemed that my realities had changed places again. Only later did I realize that the spirits had heard me calling them, despite my lack of consciousness. Dust and Snow had brought help to us.

When my father saw me standing next to him, he relaxed a bit. They helped him out of the seat and sat him in the shade. Slowly he began to drink some water. The man and woman stood aside while the shaman spoke to my father in Koori. He had studied the language and was able to speak enough with her that she understood what had happened. She also knew English. She pulled some herbs from her pockets and convinced my father to chew them. She rubbed her hands all over his head and the rest of his body, speaking in a low melodic tone. I couldn't tell if she was checking for a concussion and broken bones or projecting some of her energy into him. Perhaps it was both. After awhile my father was able to stand. The man helped him walk around the bend of the road so he could answer Mother Nature's call. He and the man then opened the hood of the OKA and managed to figure out how to get it started again.

While they were working under the hood of the OKA, the shaman spoke to me in English and asked how I was feeling. I had sat back on the ground and told her I didn't know, but that I seemed confused about what had happened. Her dark face was thin and looked like wrinkled leather. I was struck with the feeling that she had been in the desert for eons. I couldn't tell if she had any teeth. She was on her knees and moving around me. She rubbed her hands all around my head and then put her hands on my shoulders as she looked deep into my blue eyes. We were almost at eye level. She seemed to be looking clear through me into my soul. I was transfixed by her gaze and immediately felt her energy being transferred to me. She appeared to go into a trance while she spoke in Koori. It seemed to me that we had known each other forever. She then gave me some of the same herbs to chew. I felt better immediately, and after thanking the shaman, walked with her over to the OKA where my father and the other two Aborigines were standing.

This was the first time my father and I had been treated by a shaman. While it was certainly out of the norm for us, it also felt rather natural. We were out of balance with what was going on around us, and she managed to restore it. The shaman kept her eyes on me, and as I returned her gaze, I had the same feeling as when Uli rocked back and forth and looked far away. She was obviously seeing something that nobody else could see. After awhile, she said to me, "Go! Do what you must, or you'll never get any peace."

After we gave thanks all around and determined we were fit enough to drive the OKA, my father got behind the wheel. I got into the passenger seat and we drove away. I was glad there were no mountains ahead. Our new friends said they would follow for awhile to be sure the OKA continued running. They turned back after a few miles, and we all waved good-bye again.

At the next town there was a retired English physician who agreed to examine us both. He pronounced us fine and none the worse for our rough ride. That evening our baths and hotel beds felt absolutely wonderful, and we even slept in the next day. We had one more day to go before reaching Cairns. The only side trek we took that day was to stop for lunch overlooking a lake. We enjoyed

watching two black swans and their four furry hatchlings swimming around the lake. Black swans are a species unique to Australia.

The next day we joined a cruise out to the Great Barrier Reef near Fitzroy Island for my first snorkeling experience. My father was an old hand at it from his boyhood in Melbourne and couldn't wait to teach me how to enjoy the sport. Even though I was a good swimmer, I was still a bit frightened of the deep waters of the ocean. After a few minutes' hesitation, I was snorkeling all over the enclosed area. What beautiful colors the corals held, a bit more muted than shown in the film we had seen aboard the ship. There was a turtle, blue starfish, and many brightly colored fish. It was with some reluctance that we returned to the ship and our trip back to the city. After dinner, we walked on the beach and turned in early. The next day we headed to the airport for the long trip home.

When we got off the airplane at the Baltimore/Washington International Thurgood Marshall Airport, my mother, Dr. Burke, Uli and Kilmer had balloons, chocolates and flowers in their arms. We made more noise than everyone else on the flight combined. I don't remember getting and giving so many hugs at one time. My father and I had a great trip, but getting home to our family sure felt good. All six of us were talking at once while we were waiting for the luggage and during the drive home. It didn't matter. We all had lots to say and found ourselves repeating everything dozens of times later anyway. No matter how many times I told the story of our trip, I seemed to remember something new each time.

My father and I had different reactions to the search for our Aboriginal roots. He leaned more toward the historical perspective of their past, before and after the white man's arrival. He wanted to continue his research into the causes of alcoholism among the Aboriginal men. The problem had finally been recognized, and various attempts to lessen the availability of liquor and deal with the underlying issues were being met with some success. He wondered if the state of drunkenness provided a substitute for the previous generations' dreamtime experiences.

I identified more with the communication and healing abilities the Aborigines displayed. No matter how many times I tried to emulate what the Aboriginal women, especially the shamans, and a few male elders taught me, I was still not as good as they were. I could only hope to improve as time went on. I also learned that the psychic skills of the shamans were no more revered than those of the hunters, artists, dancers or boomerang makers. I thought that was probably a good thing, because the absence of class warfare had probably helped the Aborigines survive.

We turned the journals we wrote during our trip into a pamphlet for the Australian Embassy. They sold it to others interested in making the same sort of trek. Our percentage of the sales financed other trips. I wrote my journal by hand. My father kept his on his laptop computer which he powered by using the receptacle adapter in the OKA or the electric outlets in our hotel rooms. He had sent discs home via airmail so that my mother would have a copy of his journal in case anything happened to us on the way home. The portions about Aboriginal shamanism I kept for my own use. They represented part of my continuing education.

(See APPENDIX to Chapter 16 at back of book to learn about the Aboriginal flag and the Rainbow Serpent.)

Chapter Seventeen
Ottawa, Totems, and Dream Catchers

I am sure there isn't a family anywhere that doesn't have conflicts and secrets. Some just have more than others, I discovered. My mother's family had issues and conflicts that I overheard one evening while reading a book, sitting on the steps of our house. My mother didn't talk about her father very much, though she would talk at length about her mother. I never got to know my maternal grandparents, as they both died before I was born.

When my mother was in college and began learning how to conduct research, she would practice her research techniques by looking up birth and death records in the provincial courthouse. She began with her own family, just to get the feel for it. Much to her surprise, her mother was not listed as her birth mother. Her father was listed as the birth father, but her birth mother was listed as **Alice Ault**. After a while, she said to her parents over dinner one evening, "Can either of you tell me who Alice Ault is?" My grandfather became very quiet and my grandmother became a little teary. They agreed to tell her the story only if she promised to keep the information away from the rest of their family.

There was no need for the promise of secrecy. As my mother learned later, my uncles had known the real story for years. My grandfather had shared the circumstances of their half-sister's birth. Out of respect for their mother's pride, they never mentioned the conversation they had shared with their father. There was no such thing as an orphan or illegitimate child in their world. All children were entitled to be loved and have their own families. They were also happy to see their mother so contented with a new baby girl. She had a renewed purpose in her life, and she gave a lot of love to this new child. I felt lucky to be the second generation beneficiary of that love and affection.

The story I was able to put together was that my grandparents had their two sons, my uncles, early in their marriage. During a time when my grandfather attended a First Nations conference in Ottawa, the capital of Canada, my grandmother and the boys stayed at home. The conference went on much longer than expected. Away from family, and presumably lonely, my grandfather met Alice Ault, a European news reporter, and they began spending time together. When Alice became pregnant by my grandfather, she contacted him to say she did not wish to keep the baby. My grandfather and grandmother took the train to Ottawa and adopted the child, who turned out to be my mother. No wonder my mother was so crazy about my grandmother. How many women would have raised the child of her husband's illicit affair and loved that child as though she were her own? It was a saving grace that my mother filled the void my grandmother had always felt about having a girl. I always thought it curious that nobody would have ever guessed that my mother was anything but a full-blooded Native of the Americas.

I learned that Alice was Scandinavian and recalled that many Scandinavians have blue eyes. That's also when I remembered that genetic characteristics sometimes skip a generation or two and then show up again. My blue eyes had obviously manifested from recessive genes of generations back. If my Australian grandfather were to ask where my blue eyes came from now, I would have said, "Maybe from Scandinavia!" I'm grateful for my blue eyes, no matter where I got them. Most people can't see the many things and great distances with their eyes that I can with mine. I remind myself to thank my spirit ancestors for my ability to see things far away. There would be many more faraway things to see in my future.

* *

Totemism is a belief that individuals can have a direct relationship with a totem, known as a spirit being. The spirit being can be either a plant or an animal. The word itself comes from a Chippewa Indian word "ototeman," meaning relatives. My favorite poem about the Great Spirit came from Big Thunder of the Algonquin Nation.

> *The Great Spirit is in all things;*
> *He is in the air we breathe.*
> *The Great Spirit is our Father,*
> *But the earth is our mother.*
> *She nourishes us;*
> *That which we put into the ground she returns to us...*

Without anyone telling me, I knew the day would come when I would have to locate and choose my own totem. Totems are found in a variety of types. There are external totems, which choose the individual. Internal totems are chosen by an individual to reflect his or her inner nature. Helper totems happen when someone needs help. Message totems emit omens or ideas to an individual and are transitory, like helper totems.

I knew there were some external totems around me because I often felt their presence. They protected me from my mischievous nature. Like most kids, I always wanted to test the boundaries. I never had to push too far because my dreams did that for me. But how would I know when the right time to choose an internal spirit totem would be? How would I know what to choose? Would an animal just appear in front of me so I could choose it as my totem? I loved all animals, domestic and wild. How could I choose one over the other? Would it be okay if I chose more than one?

Mourning Dove, whose legal name was Christine Quintasket, from the

Salish tribe located near my mother's tribe, spoke about finding your spirit. "It was supposed that lost spirits were roving about everywhere in the invisible air, waiting for children to find them if they searched long and patiently enough. The spirit sang its spiritual song for the child to memorize and use when calling upon the spirit guardian as an adult." Maybe such a spirit was waiting around for me to snatch it from the air and take it home with me.

The Australian Aboriginal families each have a bird, a fish and an animal for their totems. The totems are reproduced as pictures rather than on totem poles. The Aborigines believe that each one of them is a reincarnation of an ancestor within his or her clan. The totems link them to the spirits of their ancestors. I learned that each shaman uses his or her own totem as a source of power.

* *

My dreams and nighttime terrors continued, no matter where I slept, until I graduated from high school. I didn't always have a lamp next to my bed when we traveled, which was every few months, so I hit upon the idea of packing my dream catcher. Some children packed a teddy bear when they traveled; I packed a dream catcher. I even hooked a small one on the chain that opened the zipper of my backpack so it was always near in case I needed some reassurance about something. I kept the small dream catcher on my backpack zipper until it fell apart at my twenty-first birthday party. I hung the larger one at the head of my bed wherever we were staying. It was the last thing I put into my bag and the first thing I took out when we arrived anywhere. It was easy to reach up and feel its comforting smooth feathers whenever my dreams awakened me. Perhaps my small dream catcher was telling me I had to face growing up, but I kept the big one and continued carrying it with me in my shaman bag every place I traveled.

According to the makers of the dream catchers, bad dreams get caught in the web while good dreams work their way through the hole in the center, rest on the feather like a dew drop, and evaporate to the Great Spirit in the morning sun. The prayer beads on the dream catcher trap all the bad dreams that are left in the web and then burn them up. I thought that was a pretty efficient way of dealing with my dreams. The bad dreams, which usually foretold some natural disaster or kept me floating into outer darkness with no return in sight, disappeared. The good ones, like participating in healing ceremonies and powwows, went to the Great Spirit. I figured the Great Spirit would return them to me whenever I needed to revisit them or remember something that my conscious mind couldn't recall.

Apparently my subconscious mind was quite creative, given the varied and exciting content of my dreams, especially the spirit beings that appeared in every form imaginable and some forms not so imaginable. Invariably, there were at least two animals in every one of my dreams, usually wild but occasionally domesticated. I always communicated telepathically with them. They became my protectors by helping me look out for danger. We always had a buddy system working, where at least one of them kept a lookout for my welfare. Sometimes the dreams left me scared after awakening, and sometimes I woke up stroking the pillow or our cat, *Cascade*, who had crawled into my bed, instead of the animal that had appeared in my dream. There were times I wished my conscious mind was as clever and creative while I was awake.

Chapter Eighteen
Trek With Kwakiutl Shamans in British Columbia

When I was seventeen, I asked Kilmer to travel with my mother and me to British Columbia. "I can't go with you because I need to work during the summer to earn money for textbooks and other incidentals," she answered. Kilmer had finished a year of college and was home for the summer. She had landed a summer job at a coffee shop near Dupont Circle in Washington, D.C. She and I packed a lot into the few weeks before my mother and I left for British Columbia. There was a lot to tell about her first year's college experience, even though we had kept in contact via e-mail. Kilmer had earned a track scholarship to Princeton University in New Jersey and had made a decision to go into sports medicine. What a perfect choice for her, I thought. She was a natural athlete, had the brains to understand the physiognomy of the human body, and was developing the skills to attend to the psychological aspects as well. Some of her counseling skills came from her college classes and some from our shamanic healing and energy work. She wanted to have a job upon graduation that would provide a decent living and have enough left over to pursue her other passion of dancing. She took the train from Princeton to New York City to see as many Broadway plays as she could fit into her busy schedule.

The teaching of dance became an avocation whenever she could spare the time. Wherever she was, she hooked up with a dance studio to provide free instruction in exchange for tuition for children who otherwise would not have had that opportunity. I promised I would e-mail Kilmer anytime I was able to locate a computer while we were in Canada. I left her at home reluctantly but was comforted by the knowledge that my mother and I were scheduled to return home before Kilmer had to leave again for college. My father decided to stay home and look after the pets and finish some projects around the house.

I never tire of the boat ride from the Vancouver, British Columbia Airport to the area farther north around Powell River where my mother's people live. My Canadian uncles were mostly retired, and their children, my first cousins, were now running their family businesses. We had done as much research as we could on the shamans of the Kwakiutl tribe, and now it was time to visit them in person. I practically had to drag my mother away from talking with the family so we could visit the shamans. The experience was nothing like what I had thought it would be.

The Kwakiutl people are concerned about cultural appropriation. Who could blame them for wanting to protect their native ways of dealing with nature? They had previously shared their way of life with other visitors. The translations were occasionally reported incompletely or incorrectly. The teachings to succeeding generations became more difficult as the children learned about their culture through film and books, rather than at their parents' knees. With her ability to speak Kwak'wala, my mother was able to override any concerns the shamans had about sharing their knowledge with me and convinced them that I was worthy of learning more about our shared heritage and healing methods.

Some words don't translate into English very well, but between my elementary Kwak'wala and the excellent English spoken by the shamans, we managed to communicate just fine. They agreed to assist in continuing my education of going into trances to "read" the bodies of people who came for healing. I learned to run my hands over people's bodies to see and feel what was inside them. Sometimes their intestines looked like garden hoses and their hearts looked like rocks during my trances. Mostly I felt and "searched" for blockages. I learned how to "extract" the blockage from the individual and throw what had been extracted into the nearest body of water to float away. When the healing ceremony was over, the "patients" were in balance with nature once again.

The first day after the healing ceremonies, I felt weak and tired. My mother sat with me to help me eat and drink to restore my strength, which returned within an hour. What a source of comfort for me. Who wouldn't feel safe with her mother nearby? After the first day, however, she no longer stayed with me during the sessions. That meant I had to learn the native ways and how to renew my energy afterwards without her assistance. I was always amazed at how exhausted I was once the trances were over and how quickly I regained my equilibrium and strength afterwards.

It was not unusual for me to travel distances thousands of miles away during the healing sessions. I learned the sacred language many shamans use, similar to speaking in tongues. I felt as though I was speaking the same language as the healing spirits. It provided an avenue for a quick penetration into unconsciousness for me and the person seeking help.

After a long hug from my mother, I traveled into the wilderness and camped outdoors for a week with my new shaman friends. It turned out to be a combination spiritual vision quest and group therapy. We often found refuge in caves and cliff overhangs. We brought food with us and each evening held a ritual of thanking the Great Spirit for our food and asking for protection. The campfires we built each evening provided easy access to shamanic trances, and we journeyed each night. After falling asleep, it was not unusual to continue the same journey previously begun before the campfire through our dreams. I remembered my childhood hero, Dr. Seuss, saying "Oh, the places you'll go!"

I didn't expect I would have to go through any life-saving experiences while surrounded by experienced shamans, but I did. Apparently, my commitment to my life's mission was still being tested. During one of the nights we were sleeping in the mouth of a cave when a grizzly bear came upon our campsite. Taking the cue from my traveling companions, I stayed still in my sleeping bag as the bear sniffed around all of us. I admit to a momentary fear of being dismembered or eaten alive. Surely this wasn't how my life was to end, was it? I worked hard at remaining still and not showing any fear because I knew he would smell it, which might prove a disadvantage. The grizzly bear actually put his paw on my shoulders, and I could hear him breathing through my sleeping bag. I could also feel his energy coming into my body. After he pawed at me for awhile, he went on to explore the rest of the campsite. Then he left the cave and disappeared. I might have known that he would return.

Upon the bear's return, I found myself talking to him as he stood in a half-standing position over me. He opened his mouth wide, and his breath came out as flames which consumed my physical body. The flames carried me to the treetops and beyond to the heavens. I called to my companions asleep far below me, but the wind blew my words away. I could feel the bear underneath me but was not afraid. At some level I knew he was taking me on a journey that would test my mettle again. We flew over the dark horizon toward the sun coming up ahead of us. As we continued traveling toward the bright sun, it became hotter and hotter. I couldn't tell if it was the bear's flaming breath or the sun closing in on me. Was this what "trial by fire" meant?

Dancing masked figures suddenly appeared in front of us. Some were wearing the thunderbird masks. I joined them in their dancing as I became the bear. I now understood the spirit language. They told me not to be afraid of becoming the bear because he would give me his great strength anytime I needed another power animal. The bear was now in my body, and I had the power of the bear. As usual, I needed that strength immediately.

The dancing ritual ended, and I began the descent back to my campsite. I became lost in the ecstasy of flying through the air. Suddenly a child appeared in front of me, holding onto a small tree just over the edge of a cliff. I had no idea that anyone else was camping in the area or that a child was near us. My shaman companions had been aroused by the child's crying. His mother and my companions were above him, trying to put a larger branch in place for him to hold onto in case the tree gave way. The child's father was trying to lower himself with a rope tied around his waist and to a larger tree higher up the cliff. The child was growing tired and would  probably soon lose his grip on the tree he was holding and tumble down the cliff.

Suddenly a bear climbed up the side of the cliff and grasped hold of the child. The bear deposited the child into the arms of the others on top of the cliff. In the barely breaking daylight it appeared that the bear then walked over to my sleeping bag and crawled inside.

I awakened to the cries of the child as the other shamans surrounded my sleeping bag. All of them knew that my body had been transformed, or shapeshifted, into a bear who was able to walk along the side of a cliff to save the child. I thought it had been a dream. Which had it been? I wasn't sure. Had I consciously shapeshifted into something else, or had the spirits done it for me?

I figured that I would probably have to shapeshift again in my life, but first, I wanted to figure out if I could do it voluntarily or if it happened involuntarily on another level of consciousness. The English word *psychic* comes from the Greek word *psyche*, which means soul or mind. Would it then follow that psychic energy means that the activity of consciousness has to do with the soul or mind and thus can be controlled?

My new shaman friends and I returned to their village where my mother was waiting. She had used the time to renew and update her indigenous counseling education. Time was drawing near for us to return home. I was suddenly eager to see my father, Uli, Kilmer, Aussie and Cascade. But we weren't able to return just yet.

I was roused out of my sleeping bag early the next morning. An illness had broken out at a Kwakiutl village farther north. I was being called to join the shamans in their travels. Two canoes were brought around, and we climbed into them for the journey upstream. I found myself rowing the canoe with great vigor and anticipation as we moved swiftly through the waters. I loved the feel of the early morning wind on my face and was oblivious to the cold. We could hear the drumming long before we arrived at the village. The elders were in a circle around a campfire, chanting and dancing. One broke away from the group and told us, "As an extra precaution, we've sent for a physician from Nanaimo." Nanaimo is a city on the eastern side of Vancouver Island. The elder continued, "We weren't sure the doctor would arrive in time to help, so in the interim, we sent for you."

As soon as we climbed out of the canoes, we were taken to several houses where we saw many ill villagers, some unable to get out of their beds. Their skin was covered with red spots. I heard one elder ask one of the shamans, "Do you think it's possible that the smallpox of a century ago could have returned?" I dreaded the answer because I thought it might be true. The World Health Organization had declared smallpox an eradicated disease in 1980, but the Kwakiutls probably wouldn't have much faith in that reassurance.

I was given a rattle and bear mask to wear as we began the healing ritual. I went into the trance quickly and danced with the others as the spirits spoke through our voices. Once we finished our chanting and dancing, each of us knelt at the sides of the ill villagers and performed extractions and the "throwing away" of their illness. It was important to throw the illness away into a nearby body of water to float away. If we did not throw the illness away, it could stay with our bodies and make us ill. We continued until all the ailing patients had been attended to, shook our hands so we would be free of the illness ourselves, and then sat back to restore our strength.

By sunset, the ill villagers had begun to rally, and many were able to take nourishment. We happily returned to our village in our canoes. My mother received word later that the physician from Nanaimo was able to take some blood samples back to his laboratory to be analyzed for pathology or disease. The report indicated a parasite in their bloodstreams. That explained why I kept seeing what looked like ants on the insides of the ill villagers during our healing ceremonies. The elders were investigating whether some fish had ingested the parasite from something that had been dumped into the waters, which then invaded the bodies of the villagers when they ate the fish. The conclusion reached by the elders was that the fish would need to be cooked for a longer period of time until all possibilities of contamination were ruled out of consideration. Once again, old and new medicine had worked together in the healing process. I felt pretty good. Maybe my shamanic healing powers, advanced and honed under the guidance of the other shamans, were beginning to work.

Chapter Nineteen
Justice for Judge O'Toole and Shamanic Wisdom

During the time my mother and I were in Canada, **Judge Gracious O'Toole** of the Court of Appeals for the District of Columbia was murdered just outside the condominium building where he lived. He had been walking from his car to the building and was killed just outside the range of the building's security camera. No evidence could be found at the crime scene to link anyone to his killing.

An immediate review of the cases over which he had presided within the past year was begun and numerous leads developed. The collective speculation of the Washington establishment was that it had probably been a revenge murder for a sentence the judge had rendered in his courtroom. Investigation of other potential motives didn't turn up any leads. The police were feeling the pressure to locate and arrest the judge's killer. Relentless and insistent press coverage about the murder went on for weeks. Judge O'Toole was from a prominent political family and had been widely touted as a possible Supreme Court nominee.

Just after my mother and I returned home, the police announced the arrest of an eighteen-year-old man and then charged him with Judge O'Toole's murder. The judge had previously sentenced the young man's brother to life imprisonment for a rival gang member's murder. Now that a motive appeared to have been found and a suspect arrested, the revenge killing speculation fit right into the rumor mill. The arrest fit a criminal justice textbook case. The picture of the arrested man was shown in every newspaper and magazine in the country, as well as on all the television channels. The entire city seemed to heave a collective sigh of relief. The police and the district attorney for the District of Columbia said it was an open and shut case. The decision was made to ask for the death penalty before the jury was even selected for the trial. At last, justice would be served. Or so it appeared.

Kilmer and I resumed our adoptive sisterhood relationship in the few weeks left to us before her return to Princeton University and my return to high school. There was so much to talk about that we came close to neglecting our daily habit of shamanic journeying. But we finally got it together and resumed our habit of journeying. During the last several years, we had begun our journeys by sitting near a window on the floor of my room with opaque eye masks over our faces, listening to the drumming tape.

The journey I took the week before Kilmer headed back to New Jersey provided some startling revelations. My journey had led me to the scene of the judge's shooting outside his building. The killer was shown to me, and it was not the young man the police had arrested for his murder. I returned from the journey greatly troubled.

We immediately talked with our parents, after which my father agreed to call the district attorney to request an appointment. After his call, my father said, "What a surprise! The district attorney wants to see us." So the next day my father, Uli, Kilmer and I took the Metro to his office in downtown Washington, D.C.

This was a whole new world for all of us. It felt like we were playing in the big leagues. After an explanation of shamanism and journeying, the district attorney proceeded to ask me everything in the world about my life. He was particularly interested in the handwritten journals I kept of my shamanic journeys. He asked in several different ways, "What percentage of incidents 'seen'

148

during a journey have turned out to be accurate and verifiable?" Neither Kilmer nor I had kept track of how many of our journeys had been acted out in real life.

After several hours, the district attorney thanked us for coming in to see him and told us he would be getting back in touch with us. We trudged to the Metro for our ride home, and for a change, all four of us were rather quiet. The meeting seemed to have unsettled all of us because we were having doubts about whether we had done the right thing in bringing the information to the attention of the district attorney.

That evening my father received a call from an assistant to the district attorney. She asked my father if I would be able to return tomorrow to work with a sketch artist. She suggested perhaps the two of us might be able to create a picture of the person "seen" during my journey. The sketch artist and I completed the work within a day, and I was pretty sure the picture we came up with was a true likeness of the man seen in my journey. Kilmer resumed packing her bags for the train trip north to Princeton. I got busy preparing for my senior year.

The media circus about the judge's murder had quieted down, or so we thought. Word somehow leaked out about the renewed search for another suspect, and the media coverage started again. For someone who was supposed to be able to predict the future, I hadn't received any psychic predictions on this case. I wondered if it was because I was focused on getting through one more year of school and making a final decision about which college to attend, along with an academic career choice, not to mention the continuation of my shamanic training. I knew what my life's work would be, but felt I somehow needed academic and medical credentials to go along with the shaman work.

Within a few weeks, another suspect was arrested for the judge's murder. The original suspect was released, and all charges against him were dismissed. As soon as the new suspect's picture flashed on the television screen during an evening newscast, I said to my parents and Uli, "That's the man; he's the one I saw in my journey." The police and the district attorney were powerless to stem the attention from the media. During that fall, the whole situation occupied many evenings of discussion at our home. Uli filled in as a surrogate for Kilmer since she was three hours away, but we kept her in the loop via e-mail. We were careful to repeat only what had been in the news.

The trial judge appointed an attorney to represent the second suspect, and the trial date was scheduled after the beginning of the year. The media was coming up with all sorts of wild conjecture about how the second suspect's identity had been discovered. I began to retreat into my shamanic journeys for guidance with the case and my part in it. The possibility of my journals being subpoenaed had just begun to enter my subconscious. After the idea bounced around in my head for about a week, the United States Marshall's Office served a subpoena on me at our front door. It was no coincidence that I was served the day after I turned eighteen.

So, my journals detailing my shamanic journeys were carted away from our house, and I was scheduled for depositions at the trial attorney's office just after Thanksgiving. My journeys to the spirits helped me put the trial out of my mind and continue my focus on my school and shamanic work.

My journals became a part of the public record of the trial. That meant anyone interested in that sort of research could go to the courthouse and review them. Part of the experience felt like a violation because the journals were a part of me. I had not written them for public consumption. As time went on, the publicity surrounding my journals would become a part of my past as I moved on to the adult world.

If the defendant was convicted of the judge's murder, I was pretty sure the press would go on to other issues. It couldn't happen quickly enough to suit me. I came to realize that my shamanic healing doesn't work well in a spotlight. My parents and Uli dropped into the courtroom whenever they could during the trial. Fortunately, my adopted grandmother, Dr. Burke, sat in the courtroom with me every single day. She was a comforting presence in the confusing criminal justice environment. Whenever the prosecuting and defense attorneys went after each other, Dr. Burke would pat my hand and whisper, "Not to worry, m'Dear, everything is going to be all right."

Despite taking over most of my life for two weeks, in reality the trial and conviction of the second suspect turned out to be little more than a distraction in the grand scheme of my life. When I saw him in the courtroom, I could feel his anger at me for revealing his identity. While planning his revenge killing of Judge O'Toole, he obviously hadn't counted on the powers of the spirit world.

The judge's widow sought me out after the trial and said in a soft voice, "For someone so young, you showed a lot of courage during your testimony, and I can feel my husband smiling down on both of us. He worked for justice and protection of innocent victims his entire life. Thank you for doing your part so that justice could be served. I'll never forget you. Now perhaps all of us can continue our journeys." She then gave me a warm embrace. Despite the glares I could feel behind my back from the perpetrator, I said a prayer that he might find forgiveness for his crime and learn a useful trade while in prison so his life afterwards could be rewarding to him and his family.

As time went on, I found that the healing powers I had learned were indeed working. Physical illness was just one of the ways to use the powers I'd been given. Often psychological issues arose for people. One was from an elderly lady whose son had died in Toronto, and she was unable to make the trip for his funeral. I asked if she wanted to travel with me in a guided shamanic journey to the site of the funeral. After the journey ended, she was very excited. She had seen her son and had held his hand as she turned him over to the Great Spirit. That experience apparently provided closure and peace for her. She died a few months later herself, and I knew she would be reunited with her son once again.

I learned how to do soul retrievals, similar to the experience with the Algonquian Indian girl in Rock Creek Park. Often people who have experienced severe trauma or near-death are unable to fully participate in their lives afterwards. Parts or all of their soul may have been left at the scene of trauma. The soul is sometimes willing to reintegrate with the person, and other times it wishes to stay where it is, usually a safer place. The shaman's responsibility is to convince the soul to return home to its proper place in the body of the ill person. Only when the ill person is completely reintegrated with all the parts of his or her soul intact can that person fully recover his or her place in the world.

Several years after his time on this earth ended in a lumberjacking accident, my Uncle Mulligan appeared during one of my shamanic journeys. I was soaring through the upper bounds of earth with a rope ladder attached to me, and he was holding onto it. He said he was ready to cross over to the light and had come to me because he needed help to get there. If he was ready to go, that could only mean he had done the hard work of handling and reconciling whatever had blocked his soul from progressing. My role was facilitating the next step. As both of us continued flying, I asked if he could see the light ahead. He said he could, and I told him to go toward the light. He hesitated, and I said he could come back and visit anytime he wanted. And with that, he was gone.

I learned how to use divination to diagnose illness. Divination is discovering hidden information through supernatural methods, such as augury (omens). Sometimes beating a drum and going on a journey will reveal a word, and the power animal or teacher can help interpret the meaning of the word in obtaining answers to questions we or others have. The journey can be used to consult the spirit of the person we're trying to heal. I learned how to use quartz crystals to really "see" what was being revealed to me. The purpose of using different divination practices is to search for clues to the causes of illness and guidance in how to proceed in healing.

I had begun to accept that my future life-saving experiences would be to save others rather than myself. Holistic medicine treats the mind, body and spirit. I constantly renewed my commitment to that concept of healing. One cannot be healed without the others also being healed. I was forced to acknowledge that realization over and over again. Wholeness meant completeness, or the totality of body, mind and spirit.

My formal education continued along that line. I obtained nursing, nurse practitioner and nurse teaching degrees in western medicine with a heavy emphasis in alternative therapies. These all complement my shaman and energy work as I travel all over the world helping the disadvantaged and ill. I utilize my clinical nursing skills and my teaching abilities, no doubt absorbed from my parents. My employment as the director of an international disaster aid agency provides the formal framework for my life's mission. Whenever a disaster strikes in the world, I'm on the next airplane to that location, serving as the administrative head organizing the relief effort. But I don't kid myself that my official work is merely a cover for my shaman work. The agency doesn't know about my work with the villagers after hours. I rationalize not telling them about it because they don't pay me for that work. Sometimes I feel like I'm living the line from the song, "Night and Day—You Are the One." At night comes spiritual healing and by day physical healing. One has to work with the other, and it's all in a day's, or a night's, work.

I also do a lot of work with the preservation of wildlife and their habitat when I travel. All those animals who visited during my vision quest wanted to be remembered. I see them every day in my mind and remember what they taught me about being mindful of the earth's sensitive balance and their place in it.

Much of my spare time is spent teaching others about the wonders and healing powers of shamanism. When counseling adolescents who have become involved in illegal drugs, I tell them I can teach them how to take a trip that will help them fly higher than any previous experience with street drugs. They learn quickly that the mind is powerful and they can stretch theirs under their own power, with no negative side effects or legal ramifications. I often receive people in my home who are looking for relief from psychic pain or physical suffering, or both. Sometimes it takes several visits to go through all the meditative journeys needed to help the ill individual become rebalanced again. If I'm not at home, I utilize a campfire or rock or a tree as my place of healing. The spirits will come anywhere they are welcomed. I set a modest basic fee for the time given and accept payment in whatever form the recipient is able to provide. Sometimes my payment is a simple "thank you." The ham shared with my family over last New Year's represented payment from a client and her family.

To keep myself balanced, I have continued the hiking pleasures begun in my youth, whether in the mountains, in the deserts, along rivers and oceans or on country roads. I hope to keep walking and observing the wonders of nature to experience inner peace and harmony until I am called back to that grand creation.

My healing gifts know no bounds, and only the Creator gets the credit. Knowing that the physical body cannot recover its equilibrium from whatever is ravaging it unless the spirit is also healed keeps me focused on both aspects in my healing work. To do otherwise would mean I was not being faithful to my calling. I may have thought I had a choice in careers, but the course had been set for me long before my time on this earth became a reality. I could not be anything but what I was created to be, nor do anything but what I was created to do. All I had to do was accept that spark of light into my being, once I figured out where the beam was pointing. It may have taken awhile to understand what my mission in life was to be, but once I started following the path partially revealed during my vision quest, I realized I could utilize the vision of a hawk anytime I needed awareness of something more than was immediately visible. The dancing animals on the train helped me remember the importance of music and dancing. The caribou, fawns and bees helped me remember the importance of every creature on this planet. The butterflies help me remember that my old self is gone forever and now, with my new wings, I must keep flying to wherever the spirits take me. The rose quartz crystals helped me remember that all things on this planet have energy and a purpose, whether minerals, animals, or vegetation. Awareness of the joy in the journey of life provides a constant connection to the Creator. My life's work is joyful, and it is guided by the hand of the Creator.

What's important is the journey itself. Life itself is an ecstatic journey for a shaman. Helping others while continuing to learn and grow ourselves is the mission of becoming a shaman. There's a reason that modern-day shamans rarely refer to themselves as shamans. That would suggest we've learned all there is to know. A shaman must keep growing in his or her work. The goal of becoming a shaman is never complete. It's important to continually reinforce the spiritual strength of a shaman. We are healers first, prophets second. Shamanic healers continue their healing journeys with humility and gratitude for their gifts all the days of their lives on this earth.

Now that I have completed the re-reading of my youthful journals that the court returned, the healing from the public exposure of the teachings from my spirit guides has come full circle. Now it's done. Another circle has closed. Once again, each day is full of the promise of more healing and spiritual renewal.

Oh, the places I've been—and still hope to go!

Epilogue

Looking back on my spiritual vision quest and training to become a shaman, I've realized the extent to which my views of life and my approaches to healing evolved. I've learned through my experiences that if strange things keep happening to you, or if you sometimes hear, see and sense things differently from others, it doesn't mean you are unbalanced or crazy. You may have more gifts than those around you. Your ability to communicate telepathically, or between minds, may be more advanced than your peers. If animals can communicate without words, why can't we? In centuries to come, it could well be the norm. Future generations may look back on verbal communication as rather primitive. It's how you react to your experiences and what you do with your gifts that matters. No one can show you your path in life. Each person has to find his or her own.

Some things remain constant. One is the importance of being good stewards of our planet, which is essential if we are to remain whole in mind, body and spirit. Another is the realization that the purpose of our time on this earth is to learn and grow spiritually. I've learned to trust my inner teacher. I've learned that we must honor the medicine that heals the body, balances the emotions, and renews the spirit. The goal of healing is both wellness and wisdom. Should you not have a human mentor in your life, you can always choose Mother Nature. She'll be good to you and good for you.

One's calling and purpose in life is sacred. Finding that path is the mission of our souls. Finding out what we've been called to be and to do during our lives on earth gives reason to our being. Whenever that passion or voice or energy arises within, then you must follow it if you hope to experience inner peace and harmony. That gentle voice is your intuition. Always pay attention and be mindful of your surroundings. If you stay fully aware, you'll hear, see, feel, taste and smell what's being communicated, even though it may not be obvious at first. Expect the unexpected. Recognize that divine spark when it happens and let it unfold around you. You'll be like a rosebud that opens and blooms.

When it comes to our search for immortality, that endless life after death, and the eternal perpetuity of our soul, I've realized that we are more alike than we are different. The color of our skin or our culture doesn't matter. Nor does it matter which spiritual path we choose while on this earth plane—whether it's through synagogues, temples, mosques, churches or the nature of the earth. It's the grand creation around us to which we all subscribe and to which we all return. We are all children of that sacred Holy Spirit, whether we call that spirit God or something else. What's important is that we maintain a connection with that force. The spiritual path we take while on this earth will lead us to our place in eternity when the time comes for us to return to that grand creation. The eternity of the universe reigns supreme, and it will be ever thus. Ah, the places we have yet to go and the things we must do before we return to you—Eternal Immortality!

Thank you for sharing this healing journey.

Peace and Light to you.

CHAPTER APPENDICES

(Further Explanation of Themes throughout the Story)

APPENDIX – Chapter Six

Didgeridoos, called "yidakis" by the Australian Aborigines, are made from eucalyptus tree branches that have been hollowed out by white ants, which we know as termites. The didgeridoo makers say, "The ants do all the hard work." The ants eat their way up through the center towards the sunlight, keeping the outer shell solid for protection against the sunlight, which would kill them. When the branch eventually dies and falls to the ground, the ends are then cut off to make the didgeridoo. The maker then turns the outside into a polished instrument. They are shipped all over the world. Didgeridoos have been called the world's oldest musical instrument. Its use is ceremonial and provides a way of studying nature. The player empathizes with the sounds of nature and reproduces the sounds through the instrument. The sound is a low droning, and you can hear alligators and elephants roaring at times. The instrument has no keys, such as a clarinet, so all the variation in the sound comes from the player changing the way he blows into it.

APPENDIX – Chapter Seven

Canada's native people, called "First Nations" in Canada, were treated only slightly better by their foreign conquerors than their brother and sister Native Americans of the United States. Many Canadian First Nations tribes were descendants of natives who had fled the United States and taken refuge in Canada. The Kwakiutl tribe was partially made up of descendants whose ancestors had traveled north from the United States and escaped to what was not necessarily a more hospitable environment. Not too long after the Europeans arrived in what became Canada in 1780, the natives were denied their ancestral lands.

Several generations later, in 1850, British Columbia's Governor James Douglas recognized pre-existing land ownership and permitted fishing and hunting. Governor Douglas was a former trader who married the granddaughter of a Cree chief. Perhaps his wife's "pillow talk" had sensitized him to the rights of the natives. Unfortunately, his successor, Joseph Crutch, began the removal of Indian children from their parents. He was known to regard the natives of his country as inferior savages. The native children were forced to attend white schools and were completely stripped of all physical reminders of their heritage. The museum pictures taken of those children during that time may have helped others realize the importance of keeping native traditions alive, because that generation of children was denied that opportunity.

In 1884, another generation later, the Canadian government outlawed the "potlatch," the major social, economic and political institution of the Pacific Northwest Coast First Nations. It was nearly seventy years before that law was repealed. It wasn't until 1992 that the government of British Columbia formally recognized aboriginal or native title and inherent right to self-government of the native peoples.

The word "potlatch" derives from the Chinook word patshatl, meaning "to give away." The Chinook were neighboring tribes of the Kwakiutl. Every person who attended the "potlatch" went home with a gift. Everyone who attended also brought something for their hosts. "Potlatches" may have been the origin of potlucks.

Mungo Martin is one of the most famous of all the Kwakiutl artists. His family was one of the few who survived the epidemic of smallpox introduced by the white man at the end of the 19th century. The disease left more than 20,000 dead, nearly wiping out the Kwakiutl nation. Mungo Martin may have done more than anyone else to preserve the totem pole and other artistic pieces of the Kwakiutl heritage. He was the first Canadian First Nations native to be awarded the Canada Council Medal for his many contributions to Canada's artistic, cultural and intellectual life. In 1956 he was commissioned by Great Britain's Queen Elizabeth II to create a totem pole marking the Provincial Centennial of British Columbia. Canada is a member of the British Commonwealth of Nations. The totem pole he created is one hundred feet high and stands in Victoria's Beacon Hill Park.

Mungo Martin lived eighty-two difficult years, long enough to see his tribe's artistry recognized throughout the world. A book on his fascinating life has been published, and his family carried on his work after his death.

In addition to totem poles, the Kwakiutls are known for killer whale artwork and thunderbird masks. There's one legend of the killer whale and the thunderbird. It would not be hard to visualize a giant bird swooping down into the river and lifting a whale in his beak, after seeing the size of the beaks 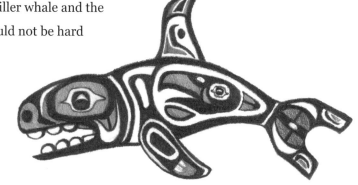 on the thunderbird masks. The story began at a time when the people could not find the salmon. They believed a whale was eating them. The thunderbird told them he would take care of the whale if they would feed him. Reluctantly, they fed the thunderbird some salmon from their dwindling stockpile. The thunderbird went down to where the river went into the lake and at the entrance picked up the whale and carried him over to the mountain and dropped him there. The salmon then started running again. The people of old probably did communicate directly with animals. Some believe that the thunderbird crowning many totem poles represents the Great Creator.

The Kwakiutl were skilled navigators and fishermen, famous for their red cedar canoes. The hull of each canoe began as a single cedar trunk. The boat builders scooped out the middle with stone tools and then steamed it into the shape of a canoe. Some of the canoes had sails. The wood of the aromatic cedar tree, because it was resistant to rot, was also used for boxes, chests and massive plank houses. The cedar bark was used to make baskets, blankets and even clothes. They were skilled plant gatherers who recognized over one hundred and forty species of plants and utilized about 95 percent of them. From the roots, bulbs, bark, sap, leaves, fruit and wood, they created food, clothing, medicine, dyes, perfumes, tools and utensils. They knew how to weave the wool from the mountain goats for clothing and how to dress the furs and skins from their hunting for clothing, drums, footwear, packs and lodge covers. They are also famous for their carving and sculpting, and their totem poles and face masks are renowned for their originality. Each home had a family totem pole depicting the family lineage, in animal form, at the

entrance. The animals represented the mythical spirits of their ancestors. Totem poles were like the coats of arms held by some families in Europe.

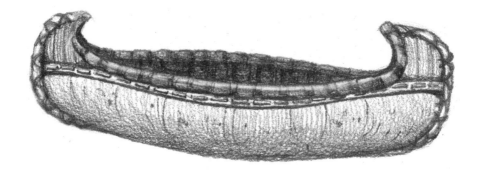

In the Kwakiutl tribe, their simple existence fostered an acceptance of both seen and unseen forces. When a Native American youth went into the forest or the desert for what was called a vision quest, he or she received instruction from a guardian spirit. Sometimes the spirits were ancestors, sometimes intermediaries between the individual and the Great Spirit. These spirits had the power to transform themselves into various visible forms. Usually, fasting and sleeplessness were rewarded by a dream or vision of the guardian spirit. That spirit would then stay with the person throughout his or her life, protecting that person from evil and guiding decisions for good purposes.

Dreams and prophecies are at the very heart of native spirituality. The spirit is believed to travel to other realms, returning with guidance that fulfills the secret desires of the soul. Strength, understanding and peace are found through inner experience, whether waking or sleeping, and the spiritual world is universal and infuses the whole natural world. It is the spiritual world that breathed life into everything on earth, like mountains and waters, and imparts a soul to every living creature born of the earth.

APPENDIX – Chapter Eight

The Medici family of northern Italy was famous for their leadership roles in the Italian Renaissance, the Roman Catholic Church and politics. One of them married the king of France and became their queen during the same years America was engaged in civil war. I think their stories would make a great movie. It may seem that all the Medicis were benevolent back in Italy, but some of them were also a bit unsavory. Some historians believe that most of them died during the bubonic plagues that killed so many people in Europe during the Middle Ages. That was but one of many plagues upon their lives. Most of the others were self-inflicted. Their lives consisted of tangled webs of power and woe, no doubt a reflection of those turbulent times.

At the end of World War II, Australia began developing as a modern nation, which required roads and dams and other structures to be built. The immigration door was opened to "displaced persons" from Europe, and my grandparents were able to book passage on one of the first ships bound for what became known affectionately as "the land down under." They must have felt lucky to be getting away from a war-ravaged country, especially since Italy wound up on the losing side of the war.

After arriving in Australia, many Italians worked with the road and dam crews, sheared sheep, drove cattle, worked at the docks and built houses. They worked at whatever was available in order to survive. Some of them were able to weave their old-world trade of working with Italian marble into their house-building talents. Their artistic ability found its way into marble fireplaces and marble patios. Many of those houses are still standing. It was only natural that many of them drifted into the restaurant and wine business, their true love. Who could have ever predicted that Australian soil would grow grapes for wine—diversified good wine at that!

During World War II, all Italians were forced to support Italy's war-time

Fascist leader, Benito Mussolini, and had no choice but to fight for their country. Australia and New Zealand lost more citizens per capita than any of the rest of the Allies in the fight against Germany, Italy and Japan.

Japanese airplanes had bombed the northern parts of Australia, probably preparing for an invasion. The American and Allied naval victories against the Japanese, especially the Coral Sea victory, may have prevented a full-scale Japanese invasion of Australia. Not only did the Australians and New Zealanders have to defend their own respective countries against Japan, but they also sent troops to Europe to fight Germany and Italy. What a twist of irony that numerous Italians had been at war against countries they later adopted.

APPENDIX ONE – Chapter Eleven

Hindus transcend the finite self through the spiritual practice of meditation. Their reservoir of being never dies, is never exhausted, and is unrestricted in consciousness and bliss.

Taoism gave us the word ch'i, which has been translated into breath, energy or the wind spirit. The Taoists draw the ch'i first into their own heart and minds and then beam it to others.

Islam began when Muhammad was visited repeatedly by the spirit of an angel. Voices of the desert sands "spoke" to him. In his world, streams and winds had their own voices.

Judaism began in the Garden of Eden with the concept of monotheism, or one God. That same God "spoke" to Abraham and told him to lead his people out of slavery. During a later time in their history, a spirit in the form of a burning bush gave Moses the Ten Commandments during his spiritual quest on Mount Sinai.

Jesus Christ and his disciples worked with the spiritual side of humans when casting out their unclean spirits to cure illnesses. The New Testament of the Bible has many references to spirits. Could that mean that when Jesus invoked the Holy Spirit for his work that he was the consummate shaman?

Shamanism can coexist with any other spiritual belief system without any conflict between them. Practicing shamanism can enhance and deepen other spiritual experiences of any form. It can be practiced by anyone who has an open, inquiring mind and a desire to improve his or her spiritual life. Shamanism often begins as a personal revelation and inner healing, evolves into a desire to bring balance and healing into the individual's world, and then progresses into the larger earth system.

Every culture possesses creation myths, from the Australian Dreamtime to the Biblical story of Genesis to the Greek Uranus (sky) and Gaia (earth) story to the Indian Hindu and Japanese Shinto Golden Eggs being split into heaven and earth, and even to the Big Bang theory. These are energetic forces at work that are difficult to understand and relate to one's everyday existence. The physical world and the spiritual world constantly intermingle.

Ancestor worship or contact with the spirits of the departed was apparently the earliest form of worship for many races and cultures. Ancient peoples often slept on top of the graves of their ancestors in an effort to receive their wisdom. Could spiritualism be based on the belief that humans survive death intact and communicate with the spirits of the deceased? If we are in fact spiritual beings enjoying a temporary journey in a physical body on earth, then surely it is important to attend to our spiritual needs, individually and collectively.

APPENDIX TWO - Chapter Eleven

Among the Australian Aborigines, the Dreamtime explains the origins and culture of the land and its people. Any previously living being, animal or plant continued to exist in spiritual form once he returned to the earth or ascended into the sky. Ancestor spirits came to earth in human and other forms. Dreamtime is known as "time before time" or "the time of the creation of all things." Everything that had been associated with living beings, animals or plants during their lifetimes left a vibrational residue in the earth. The characters and events of the Dreamtime set up a pattern or way of life for the Aborigines to follow. It was only in extraordinary states of consciousness that they could be aware of, or attuned to, the inner sacredness and dreaming of the earth. Rituals sprang up to maintain laws and relationships and to help the Aborigines keep in touch with the Dreamtime beings.

Aborigines believe that all forms of life are conscious, that they can be spoken to and are aware of what happens. Trees and hills can hear and places can be happy or sorrowful. The songs of the Aborigines become their vehicle of communication. The songs come to them through their spiritual bodies. While their bodies sleep, their spirits exit through their navel and fly off to a distant land. During their travels, their spiritual bodies find themselves at a ceremony where they hear the songs, memorize them, and then return to their still-sleeping body.

Aboriginal Dreamtime is tuned to receiving images, suggestions, the pulsating voice of the earth, as well as the echoes of the Creative Ancestors in the heavens. It was the Creative Ancestors' understanding of space and the ability to establish their sense of place while in a state of wandering that gave them a human and spiritual dimension.

The Australian Aboriginal shamans described celestial ascents to meet with the sky gods, similar to the more recent UFO abduction stories. The shaman was chosen either voluntarily or spontaneously, was set upon by spirits, ritualistically killed and then experienced a wondrous journey to meet the sky god. After the shaman is restored to life, a new life as the tribal shaman begins.

In the book of poems, *Message stick: contemporary Aboriginal writing*, a poem written by **Nellie Green** helped me understand Dreamtime.

Dreaming Tracks Lead Me Wandering

Dreaming tracks lead me wandering
Songs speaking along treasure trails

Holding mysteries of our mothers and fathers
The reddened Earth remembers days
Of a different time

Still, the sacredness needs no harness,
Only honesty
Precious places shouldn't need promise of prevention
But rather, affection

The pain is experienced but not expected
And one more drop of blood seeps from the
Skies into the sand
As wisdom races with the winds scattering
The seeds of the Spirits
Spirits longing to live, yet dismissing their delusions

And not counting their losses.
By Nellie Green

Imagine what it must have been like living as an Aboriginal native in a country with a history of probably fifty thousand years, all the while assuming their people were the only ones on the earth. Suddenly the ocean waves began delivering ships carrying light-skinned people who looked and acted differently.

The new people wore clothes on their bodies, even in the extreme heat of the Australian Outback, and spoke a language unknown to the natives. As the new people followed the rivers and explored further into the heartland of Australia, they interrupted centuries-old hunting territories and waterholes. The Aborigines had depended on the hunting grounds and waterholes for survival. The Europeans brought with them epidemics of smallpox and measles which nearly destroyed some communities. Sexual contact brought venereal diseases to the Aborigines. The age-old question arises once again. Why do people who think they are civilized look with such contempt on people who have been observing their native customs and thriving just fine for thousands of years?

Historians who wrote about the European discovery and populating of Australia during the 18th and 19th centuries noted that the Aborigines tried to incorporate the Europeans into what they felt was their superior native system of exchange and hospitality. The Europeans adopted the opposite tactic but realized quickly that the Aborigines had little interest in assimilating into their culture. To their credit, some Europeans appreciated and even revered the native way of life. They listened to their Dreamtime stories and understood how their artwork told the stories of their civilization.

As the Europeans quickly discovered, the heartland of Australia was not fertile, as is the case in the United States. Their interior was mountainous and desert-like. Gigantic volcanic and other forces of nature had once been at work creating the continent of Australia. Most of the fertile land in Australia is located in the southeastern portion of the country. That's where the majority of the vineyards and farms are located and where most of the people in the country live. Australia is almost the same size as the continental United States. It looks smaller on our world globe, but that may be because it's completely surrounded by water, unlike the United States.

After awhile, it became clear to the Aborigines that the Europeans would not be moving on and that they wanted to own the land the natives had farmed and hunted for centuries, rather than share it. Any prospects of bargaining with the new settlers evaporated in the face of their fences and guns.

APPENDIX – Chapter Thirteen

When Black Elk, the Oglala Sioux shaman and holy man, was a very old man, someone asked him to record the story of his life. I've listened to the story on tape lots of times. Whenever I sat in our meditation circle, I was reminded of what Black Elk said about circles:

"You have noticed that everything an Indian does is in a circle, and that is because the Power of the World always works in circles, and everything tries to be round. . . . The sky is round, and I have heard that the earth is round like a ball, and so are all the stars. The wind, in its greatest power, whirls. Birds make their nests in circles, for theirs is the same religion as ours. Even the seasons form a great circle in their changing, and always come back again to where they were. The life of a man is a circle from childhood to childhood, and so it is in everything where power moves."

Life does appear to take place in a circle. Black Elk, a survivor of the Wounded Knee massacre, spent most of his adult life as a healer and lived until 1950.

APPENDIX – Chapter Sixteen

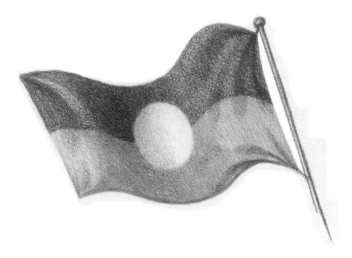

The Aborigines of Australia have their own flag. In the middle of the Aboriginal flag is a yellow sun which represents yellow ochre, found naturally in the earth and in the sun, the giver of life. The red rectangle behind the bottom half of the sun represents the red earth and the spiritual relationship the Aborigines have to the land. The black background represents the Aboriginal people.

In Australian Aboriginal legend, the Rainbow Serpent is the most powerful of all the totems. He created the waterways and rivers as he wiggled across the land. His movement pushed up the earth, creating the hills and mountains. One anthropologist believes the rainbow serpent is the connecting link between the transcendental, or supernatural and totemic, natural power.

The End